The
Christmas
Nutcracker

Ballerina Dreams

Collect all the books in the series:

Poppy's Secret Wish

Jasmine's Lucky Star

Rose's Big Decision

Dancing Princess

Dancing with the Stars

Dancing Forever

The Christmas Nutcracker

Ballerina Dreams

The Christmas Nutcracker

Ann Bryant

USBORNE

My sincerest thanks to Janet Lewis, Victoria
Zafiropoulos, Matz Skoog, and Tracy Falcone
for all their invaluable help.

The publisher would like to thank Sara Matthews of the
Central School of Ballet for her assistance.

First published in the UK in 2005 by Usborne Publishing Ltd.,
Usborne House, 83-85 Saffron Hill, London EC1N 8RT, England.
www.usborne.com

Copyright © 2005 by Ann Bryant

The right of Ann Bryant to be identified as the author of this work has been asserted
by her in accordance with the Copyright, Designs and Patents Act, 1988.

Cover photograph by Ray Moller.
Illustrations by Tim Benton.
The name Usborne and the devices ♀ 🌐 are Trade Marks
of Usborne Publishing Ltd. All rights reserved.

A CPI catalogue record for this title is available
from the British Library.

UK ISBN 0 7460 7027 6

First published in America in 2006. AE
American ISBN 0 7495 1369 7
FMAMJJASOND/06

Printed in India.

The Story of
the Nutcracker

Many years ago on Christmas Eve in a little town in Germany, guests were arriving for a party at the house of a doctor and his wife and their two children, Clara and Fritz. The children's godfather, Councillor Drosselmeyer, who was an inventor of mechanical toys, entertained everyone at the party with magic tricks and showed off his new toys, including a mechanical castle. He also had a very special gift for Clara, a nutcracker doll in the shape of a soldier. Clara was delighted

with her present, but Fritz thought it was stupid and snatched it away from her. As he ran off, the nutcracker fell to the floor and the grown-ups were angry with Fritz. Clara picked up her precious nutcracker and laid it gently in her dolls' cradle.

A little later, Councillor Drosselmeyer read all the children an exciting story called The Nutcracker and the Mouse King. Then all the guests went to dinner but Fritz stayed behind, and when he was sure no one was watching, took the nutcracker out of the cradle and put it in the mechanical castle.

That night Clara couldn't sleep, so she crept downstairs to find the nutcracker doll. In the dark living room, Clara saw some very strange things happening. An army of mice was attacking the toy soldiers in the castle, and the leader of the army, a terrible Mouse King with seven heads, was fighting the nutcracker. Their long swords clashed together and Clara hardly dared watch. It looked horribly as though the Mouse King was getting the better of the nutcracker, so Clara bravely rushed in to try and help him. Instantly the nutcracker turned into a handsome prince, who then killed the Mouse King. In a flash the rest of the mice and the soldiers vanished.

The prince wanted to thank Clara so he took her on a magical journey through the Land of Snow to his homeland the Kingdom of Sweets. There, Clara was crowned a princess and invited to sit on a throne as the guest of honor at a feast of dancing. She watched the Sugarplum Fairy and the prince dance, then there was a Spanish dance, an Arabian dance, a Chinese dance, a dance for Reed Pipes, one for Bonbons and lastly the beautiful Waltz of the Flowers.

Then all the dancers were wildly spinning and whirling together faster and faster, before they slowly began to disappear. Clara felt her dream melting away, and when she opened her eyes she was all alone, with her treasured nutcracker beside her.

1 Poppy

Hi! I'm Poppy. And I'm the luckiest girl in the world. Well, actually, I'm one of the twenty-two luckiest girls in the world. You see, I'm about to go to London for my first rehearsal of the *Nutcracker* with a big professional ballet company. I still can't believe that I was chosen at the audition, and I'm so, *so* excited.

I'm a student at the Coralie Charlton School of Ballet, and Miss Coralie, the Principal, is the greatest teacher ever. My best friends, Rose and Jasmine, think so too. Miss Coralie used to be a soloist with the Royal Ballet Company so she's got very high standards. She's also very strict and works us students really hard.

"She's here! I can see her car pulling up!" I shouted up to Jasmine, who instantly came flying downstairs with her ballet bag, and a big smile on her face.

Rose was jumping up and down with excitement. "I can't believe she's actually come to see us off!"

That wasn't strictly true. Miss Coralie knew Jasmine's mom was taking us up to London on this first day of rehearsals and she'd promised to drop by to wish us luck on the big day as she was passing Jasmine's house.

Jasmine opened the door and we all stood there, totally tongue-tied.

"Ready for a very special experience, girls?" Miss Coralie asked in her soft, clear voice.

We all nodded hard and I couldn't help staring at her. We hardly ever see her out of her ballet clothes, but whenever we do, it's easy to tell that she's a dancer, because she's so slim and strong with her straight back and her turned-out feet. Every move she makes is graceful and when she smiles you imagine her on a stage with her big eyes in a perfect face that looks as though someone's carved it out of marble. Today, though, her face looked paler than usual and I thought her eyes seemed a little tired too.

"Come in, come in," said Jasmine's mom, appearing at the door.

"No, I won't hold you up." Miss Coralie smiled. "I just wanted to wish the girls the best of luck." She looked carefully at each of us and spoke gently but firmly. "I know you'll do me proud."

We nodded again and promised to try our very best.

"And I'll be there in the audience on Christmas Eve to see you in your first performance," she added.

A lovely excitement welled up inside me. I'd

already thought that this Christmas would be the best ever, but now I knew it was going to be by *far* the best.

"What a beautiful lady!" sighed Jasmine's mom as Miss Coralie got back in her car. Jasmine's mom is French and very dramatic. She looked at her watch. "Time to go. Now, you're sure you've got everything, yes?"

The three of us got into the backseat of the car, but we didn't talk at first. I think we were all thinking about Miss Coralie and what an amazing ballet teacher she is. If it hadn't been for her strict teaching and high standards we wouldn't be on our way to our first rehearsal of the *Nutcracker* right now. That thought sent a big shiver of excitement and nervousness racing through my veins and got me thinking back to the time when Miss Coralie first told our grade-five class about the auditions.

"*Ballet Theater UK*," she explained, "will be holding auditions in London for ballet students, boys and girls, from the whole country who would like to dance with their company in the *Nutcracker* at Christmas time. The performances will be from Christmas Eve to mid-January, including lots of matinees, at the Princess Theater in London."

When Miss Coralie first told us this incredible news, I remember the hairs on my arms standing up because I was so excited at the thought of dancing in a real professional company. And the *Nutcracker* is such a Christmassy ballet that it would just be the most magical thing *ever* to be able to dance in it.

I knew that if I passed the audition it would mean lots of trips back and forth to London for all the rehearsals, and I was slightly worried in case my parents said it was out of the question because of all the time and expense. Rose was anxious about that too, but poor Jasmine was the most worried of the three of us, because her dad's so strict about schoolwork, and we knew that the *Nutcracker* rehearsals started during the last week of term, which would mean missing school that week.

At first it felt like a miracle had happened when all of our parents said it was fine for us to audition. It was especially wonderful that Jasmine's dad didn't seem to mind.

"I can't understand it," Jasmine said. "He's just so relaxed about it all." But then her face fell. "Oh I get it," she added in scarcely more than a whisper. "He doesn't think I'm good enough to pass, so there's not much chance of me missing school."

Then Rose and I started to wonder if all our parents were secretly thinking the same thing, and in the end I asked my mom.

"Poppy," she said, "there are going to be hundreds and hundreds of girls auditioning. You mustn't get your hopes up, or you'll only be disappointed."

And then we'd started a new worry. It was

Rose who'd dared to say the words out loud. "What if one of us gets in, but the other two don't?"

"I *know*," Jasmine and I said at exactly the same time, in the same anxious voices.

"Look!" cried Jasmine's mom, bringing me back to the here and now. "Christmas trees! I'll pick one up on the way back from London."

"And can we decorate it when I get home?" asked Jasmine, leaning forward.

"Let's wait till the weekend," said her mom, "when you won't be so tired."

In the back of the car we three smiled at each other. Dancing in the *Nutcracker* with the first performance on Christmas Eve and Miss Coralie in the audience, then Christmas itself the next day. Everything felt so totally perfect.

Jasmine's mom dropped us off at the *Ballet Theater UK* rehearsal studios, and as soon as I set eyes on the big, old, red-brick building I started feeling jittery, because this was where we'd auditioned. Someone came to meet us at the door and took us to the changing room. She introduced herself as Sue, and told us she would be looking after us during the rehearsal time, and that she was called a chaperone. We all felt shy, but at least we three knew each other. There were a few girls there who didn't know anyone at all. So we started to get changed and the rest of the girls gradually arrived. A girl called Tamsyn, who also goes to Miss Coralie's, was the last to turn up. At Miss Coralie's she always shows off about how supple she is and what a good dancer she is, and I wondered whether she would be the same here at *Ballet Theater UK*.

Once we were all changed, Sue said she wanted us to walk around the room shaking hands with each other and introducing ourselves, while remembering as many names as possible.

"It's an excellent way of getting to know one another," she said, smiling at all of us.

There was one girl, though, who didn't even ask my name. She just told me she was called Amelia Kent and that she had danced with *Ballet Theater UK* last year. Then she leaned forward and sneered, "The chaperone was much younger than Sue, and didn't treat us like babies either."

At the end of the introductions, Sue explained that there are two chaperones and that the other one is responsible for the boys, who have their own changing room. "Our job is to look after you students," she said, "and make sure you're dressed correctly and are always in the right place at the right time..." Then she gave us all a stern look. "And, of course, that you behave yourselves!"

I saw Amelia roll her eyes and start fiddling with her hair in front of the mirror.

"What do you think of Amelia?" Rose whispered to me and Jasmine when Sue had finished talking.

"Didn't really like her," I whispered back, as my eyes strayed over to where Amelia was still looking at herself in the mirror. She had pale gold hair scraped back into the tightest bun I'd ever seen. She also had big blue eyes and a perfect dancer's body with long legs, narrow hips and a slim, straight back.

"She was in *Cinderella* last year," whispered Rose.

"I know... She must be really good," I admitted.

"Have you seen who she's talking to now?" asked Jasmine, pushing in one of Rose's hairpins for her. "Tamsyn."

Rose rolled her eyes and grinned. "Do you think we should warn Amelia?"

I couldn't help smiling. Tamsyn totally hates it if anyone gets more praise and attention than her.

"Anyone need any more help with hair or anything?" said Sue, and we shook our heads.

Then, while she checked that our leotards, tights and shoes were neat and clean, we all stood perfectly still and no one made a sound.

"Good!" she said when the inspection was over.

Rose must have been holding her breath without realizing it because she suddenly let it out in a really noisy sigh and several people snickered. Normally, things like that don't bother Rose in the slightest, but even *she* must have been feeling nervous because I saw her bite her lip and glance at Sue to make sure she hadn't done anything wrong.

Next, Sue explained about the rehearsals. "You all met Miss Farraday, the ballet mistress, at the auditions. Well, she will be attending all rehearsals. You'll also recognize Mr. Rivas from the auditions. He's a very important person – the artistic director. The other person who will be there is Miss Porter, the choreologist..."

"Don't you mean *choreographer*?" Tamsyn interrupted.

Sue didn't exactly sigh, but she paused before she answered, and I think she was a little irritated, even though she didn't show it. "No, I mean *choreologist*. Miss Porter's job is to know precisely where everyone should be on every single count of the music. The *choreographer,* Don Crowther, is here today too. He won't necessarily come to all the rehearsals though. You're allowed to call him Don...if you need to speak to him at all, that is."

I gave Jasmine a sideways glance to see if she looked as terrified as I felt, but she was staring right ahead. I wasn't surprised. Jasmine always pays attention and does what she's supposed to do, and never goes off into dreams like me, or plays around like Rose. No wonder she's such a good dancer. She's got the best discipline out of the three of us.

"Excuse me..."

Sue had turned to lead us out of the changing room through to the rehearsal studio, but she stopped and turned back when she heard Tamsyn's voice.

"Do we call Miss Farraday and Miss Porter – and what's that other one – by their first names?"

Someone gave a little snort as if to say, *what a stupid question*, and I saw that it was Amelia.

"No, you call them Miss Farraday, Miss Porter and Mr. *Rivas*," said Sue firmly. "Don Crowther is a guest choreographer and not part of the artistic staff at *Ballet Theater UK*. But that doesn't mean that you can be disrespectful, of course." She paused and raised her eyebrows. "Any more questions?"

If I'd been spoken to like that I wouldn't have said another word because it had sounded like Sue was putting Tamsyn in her place, but Tamsyn didn't seem to notice. "We *can* call the actual professional dancers by their first names, though, can't we?" she said in her usual loud voice.

"There really won't be time for talking to the professional dancers," said Sue, sounding impatient now. "They'll be concentrating hard on learning their roles too, and you mustn't distract them."

"Will they be here today?" asked a girl, who I think was called Sasha.

"No, dear. The first few rehearsals are for you students alone, so you can learn all the steps." Sue glanced at her watch. "Now we really must go. Follow me and don't talk."

This part reminded me of Miss Coralie's. We always have to be quiet when we're lining up outside class. Sue led us down a hallway, and I heard another door open behind us and turned around to see the boys following us silently with their chaperone. I looked out for Kieran, who's another student of Miss Coralie's. He grinned at Rose and she gave him a thumbs-up, because she knows him better than Jasmine and I do. Then we all went through some double doors and around a corner, where Sue suddenly stopped. She turned around and put a finger on her lips to make sure we were all silent, before opening a door to show a beautiful big studio. Immediately, light flooded into the hallway and made a swarm of butterflies flutter around my stomach.

Amelia was at the front of the line and didn't hesitate at all, just marched right in. I suppose she felt confident because of having done it last year. If it had been me at the front, I would have tiptoed in on shaky legs and hoped that someone would go ahead of me.

"Come on in, that's right," said the man who'd been at the auditions. So this was the artistic director – Mr. Rivas.

I recognized Miss Farraday from the audition too. She and Mr. Rivas were poring over some papers together. She looked up quickly and gave a sort of distracted smile, then frowned back at the papers, with her pen jabbing away on whatever was written there. Another man, who must have been the choreographer, Don Crowther, was wearing sweatpants and a vest top and didn't even look at us as we trooped in. He was deep in thought, his hands moving in the same pattern as his dancing feet. It's called marking when you dance something through roughly like that.

"Sit down here," Sue told us all in a low voice, "and wait quietly until someone is ready to talk to you." Then she hurried out.

I sat down next to Jasmine and Rose, and watched the pianist. I'd always thought that Mrs. Marsden, who plays the piano at Miss Coralie's, was the best pianist in the world, but this man seemed like a magician, the way his fingers rattled up and down the piano keys, only pausing for a split second to slap the page of music over. I've got the CD of the *Nutcracker,* so I recognized the music. It's one of my favorite pieces.

"Can I have the beginning of that section once more, Andy?" said the man in the sweatpants to the pianist.

"That must be Don Crowther," Jasmine whispered.

Andy started playing the same music that we'd had at the audition, and it immediately brought the memories flooding back.

The audition had been like a real class with about fifty students, including Jasmine, Rose and me. It had taken place in another studio in this same building. Miss Farraday had been at the class, and Mr. Rivas had watched carefully too.

I can't remember a single thing about the first twenty minutes because of being so nervous. I just remember that when we stopped doing set steps and were told that we could improvise any steps we wanted, I'd felt so happy. It was as though I'd been dancing up to my waist in a lake up until that moment, with my legs struggling to move against the weight of the water, but then it had suddenly all evaporated and I was dancing freely.

The pianist had filled the room with his music and I'd filled the room with my dancing, because there were only four students at a time dancing in this part of the audition, so it felt like I had all the space in the world. Even when the last note had faded away, it was as though I was still on the highest cloud, hearing the music in my head. Mr. Rivas had looked at me for such a long time that in the end I'd turned red. And that was when he'd suddenly said, "Right, thank you. Next group." And I'd come out of my dancing dream and scuttled back to my place feeling embarrassed *and* on top of the world. Later, when we went off to be collected by our parents, another group of students arrived. Apparently, the auditions went on for two solid days.

"Okay, let's get started."

And now I was being pulled out of my

dancing dream for the second time, right back to the here and now, because another member of the ballet had come into the studio and all four adults were standing in front of us.

My heart started to beat a little faster. It had suddenly hit me that the rehearsal was about to begin, and from this moment on I had to prove that I was as good as they'd thought I was at the auditions. That was scary because I felt sure it must have only been the free dance that had gotten me through the audition. But now I was going to have to learn complicated sequences of steps and remember placings and positions and make sure I used my best technique the whole time. I shivered.

It was all right for Jasmine. She had the brain to remember sequences of steps, and her technique was amazing. And Rose and Tamsyn were the most flexible girls in Miss Coralie's and both were really good at turning out. People always said I had good expression in my dancing, but that's not as important as the other things when you're learning a new dance. What if the adults here realized they'd made a mistake and decided I wasn't good enough after all? I kept on thinking about what Mr. Rivas had said at the end of the auditions. "Remember, please, that even those of you who pass the audition are always on trial and if either your attitude or your dancing is unsatisfactory, you can easily be replaced."

I had to tell myself to stop worrying and being silly, and start focusing, because Don, the choreographer, was talking.

"Okay, everybody. I'm sure you all know the story of the *Nutcracker*, so now I'm going to explain how you, the students, will fit into *our* particular interpretation of the ballet, and as I'm talking, I'd like you to picture the scenes. Feel the magic. Close your eyes if it helps."

I glanced around to check whether the others were closing their eyes, and saw that most of the boys, including Kieran, had just put their heads down and were staring at the floor. But nearly all the girls had closed their eyes, so I did too, and the characters came to life as Don talked.

"In the Christmas party scene at the start of the ballet, I want the characters of the children to come through, as well as their excitement about Christmas. But it's not just about acting – otherwise this might as well be a play. I've choreographed this scene fairly densely. That is to say, there are lots of steps to learn and a lot of individual responsibility to be taken. For example, when Drosselmeyer has shown off his mechanical dolls, one of the children imitates the stiff jerky action of the dolls, to amuse her friends. This will be a difficult solo, and whoever we choose to do it will have to be very flexible indeed." Don chuckled. "The word 'challenging' springs to mind!"

I hugged my knees when I heard that because I thought it sounded fantastic, and I was just imagining how good Rose would be as the mechanical doll because she's incredibly flexible.

"So, in Act One," Don went on, "each of you will *either* take the part of a child at the party, *or* of a mouse in the battle scene with the soldiers."

I was hoping like crazy that I'd be chosen as one of the children at the party, but there was no time to think about that because Don was going on to tell us about the second part of the ballet.

"In Act Two, which takes place in the Kingdom of Sweets, Clara watches all the different dances, and I want the stage to both look and feel like the most magical place that ever existed. Our costumes and scenery are stunning and I expect our dancing to be *equally* stunning. Some of you students will have a role in the *Bonbons* dance, in which the choreography is simple but effective, so you must perform the steps absolutely perfectly.

Some of you will be in the *Mirlitons* dance, which again is simple but strong, and both these dances are for students only. The remaining few of you will be in the *Waltz of the Flowers,* which is a very demanding dance for both students *and* professional dancers. I nearly choreographed the dance for the professionals only, but I decided to give the students a chance and I'm hoping that it will be exquisite."

I love the word "exquisite". It means perfectly beautiful and expressive. It would be the best thing ever if I were chosen for this dance because *Waltz of the Flowers* is my very favorite music in the world.

"The end of the ballet will be a positive whirlwind, when all the dancers come together," said Don. "It will also be very tricky to rehearse, but I'm sure we'll manage it if everyone is prepared to try their hardest, one hundred percent of the time."

I opened my eyes and looked around in a

daze, but immediately snapped out of it because Miss Farraday, the ballet mistress, was talking now.

"All right, listen up. As Don said, there are two acts in *Nutcracker*. Every one of you will be dancing two different roles – one in Act One and one in Act Two. There are only twenty children needed in each performance, but there are forty of you here because, of course, there are two casts."

My heart started banging and I could feel my face turning pale because I hadn't realized there were going to be two different casts. I immediately looked at Jasmine and Rose and saw that they hadn't realized either, and then I was sitting up as straight as I could, not that that would make any difference now because the two casts must have already been decided. It was just that I was desperate for Rose, Jasmine and me to be in the same cast, dancing in the same performances.

"I'll read out the names in alphabetical order

of those students in the *first* cast." And before I knew it she'd said, "Jasmine Ayed, Rose Bedford..." I held my breath. *Please let it be me too. Please let it...* Amelia Kent's name was read out and that's when I felt Jasmine reaching for my hand. She wanted to do a thumb-thumb, which is when we all three press our thumbs together for good luck. I felt for Rose's hand. She pressed her thumb against mine and we sat there holding our breath. But it didn't work. The next thing I knew, Miss Farraday was saying, "Okay then, the rest of you are in the second cast."

In the row in front of me, Tamsyn's shoulders drooped. She was obviously wishing she'd been chosen for the first cast too. Kieran would be in the second cast with me, but that wasn't anything like the same as having Jasmine and Rose. But then a huge spark of happiness made me feel a hundred times better, when Miss Farraday announced which roles we'd all be dancing, and it turned out that Jasmine, Rose and I had all been chosen as children at the Christmas party in Act One, and dancers in the *Waltz of the Flowers* in Act Two.

"'Scuse me," said Tamsyn, sticking her hand up.

Miss Farraday looked surprised that anyone was asking a question. "Yes...?"

"Are we allowed to swap casts if we want?"

I saw a look pass among the adults. It was Mr. Rivas, the artistic director, who answered Tamsyn in a quiet voice.

"Absolutely not. The casts have been selected carefully. It's all about coloring, height, the way you dance... But I must stress that the first cast is no better than the second. Both are equally good." Then he suddenly turned even more businesslike. "Let's get started. First, warm-up."

For the second time that morning, I told myself to stop being silly. It wasn't the end of the world that I wouldn't be dancing with Rose and Jazz. I was amazingly lucky to have got into the

Nutcracker in the first place, and I had to keep remembering that.

But there was still a little shadow hanging over me about that, and I knew I'd have to talk to myself many more times to make it go away.

2 Rose

Hi! I'm Rose. And right now I'm doing the thing I love best. Dancing. Rehearsing the *Nutcracker*, to be precise. I don't think I've ever concentrated so hard in my whole life. Miss Coralie would be really proud of me if she could see me now. And actually, so would my teachers at school. Mmm...what a lovely thought. You see, Poppy, Jazz and I are missing the last week of this semester because of *Nutcracker* rehearsals. Yessss!

I never realized how precisely dancers have to learn everything. Imagine you've been told to do some steps and you've got to finish up in a certain place, and you think you're standing in exactly the right spot, but it turns out that you're a few inches out. Well those few little inches are very important because they affect all the other dancers. The teachers here are very strict about things like that, especially Miss Porter, the choreologist.

Today is Saturday the seventeenth of December, the third day of rehearsals, and we're still rehearsing separately from the professional dancers. Mr. Rivas and Miss Farraday said we students are learning the steps on our own first, so as not to waste a single second of the dancers' time when they join in with us. I'm already nervous about dancing with real professionals, and I don't usually get nervous about anything.

So far we've spent most of our time rehearsing Act Two of the ballet, but today we're concentrating on the Christmas party scene in Act One. I'm supposed to be a very lively child, who arrives at the Christmas party with her brother, her mother and father.

I'm dying to meet the dancer in the role of Clara. You see, Clara is the main child in the story, but it's such a big part that it has to be a professional doing it, and apparently the dancer they've chosen is tiny – only a little taller than Poppy. She's called Lisette Canning. Amelia told me that. I think she asked Miss Farraday. Amelia is very relaxed about talking to the adults. I suppose it's because she was here last year. It gets on your nerves the way she keeps dropping that into the conversation.

Right now, Miss Porter is going over the part where one of the children at the party is imitating the jerky wooden movements of a mechanical doll. It's supposed to be comical and I think the choreography is amazing. It's Sasha who has this role in the first cast and Tamsyn in the second. Sasha seems to be struggling a little because the steps are so hard.

"Make it very jaunty, Sasha," said Miss Porter encouragingly. "That's right…"

Don stepped forward to stand beside Miss Porter and join in the encouragement. "Really jerky as you come up with a straight back…and *développé* with the right leg…"

Between them, Miss Porter and Don kept talking Sasha through the whole sequence of steps until she dropped into the sideways splits at the end, her head on one side and her palms up.

"Good!" said Miss Porter. "It's very tricky indeed. Let's have another try."

It was obvious that the rest of us weren't needed at that moment so I went off to the side to do some stretching exercises. I noticed that Miss Farraday was at the other end of the studio going over the doll part with Tamsyn, who is dancing that same difficult solo in the second cast.

Don was frowning and tapping his chin with

his finger as he watched Miss Porter working with Sasha, and I was wishing like crazy that *I* was Sasha because I felt sure I could do the steps. I sighed a little as I put my right leg up on the *barre* and leaned my body over it. Then just when I was about to slide my leg along the *barre* to stretch it farther, I heard Amelia speaking to me in an urgent whisper. "What are you doing, Rose?"

"I'm stretching."

"Look, I know this is your first time dancing with *Ballet Theater UK*," she said in a bossy voice, "but I can tell you, Miss Porter and the others prefer you to stay focused and watch what's going on during rehearsal. You don't want people to think you're showing off, do you?"

"Why would they think that? I'm just stretching."

Amelia looked suddenly angry. Her face was turning all red. "It's like you're trying to prove that you're more flexible than Sasha, and you want someone to notice you and give you her part," she hissed.

Well, that did it. I quickly pulled my leg off the *barre* and stood completely still. The last thing I want is for anyone to think I'm a show-off. Poppy and Jazz and I had only just been talking the night before about how awful it would be if any of us were thrown out and had to be replaced by a reserve.

"Okay, listen up, everyone," said Miss Porter. "I want to show Don a complete run-through of this section with the first cast, then we'll swap casts. For the moment, Mr. Rivas and Miss Farraday are going to dance the roles of Clara and Fritz's parents. Right, positions please..."

The room went quiet apart from the swishes and plips of ballet shoes. Then a few seconds later, when we had all found our places, and the second cast students were sitting down to watch, it was completely silent.

"And *three* and *four* and…"

The piano music began, and off we went. I felt like a small cog in a big wheel as I pretended to run away from a boy called Dominic, who's playing the part of my brother, then I twirled around with Amelia and did a little sequence of *pas de bourrées* and *echappés* with Jazz and a few others. After that I had to run in a certain pattern all over the stage, before ending up in the line of children waiting to be given a Christmas present. I concentrated really hard and got the best feeling when everything fitted so perfectly. The only part that wasn't right yet was Sasha's tricky solo.

"Well done," said Don to us all, at the end. He rubbed his chin and looked up at the ceiling deep in thought, while we stayed still as statues, only our breathing disturbing the silence.

We weren't sure if we were supposed to be running off so that the other cast could take our places, but Don was frowning hard at the floor now, and the rest of the adults weren't moving. Finally, he told everyone to come and sit down, then he asked the ballet mistress, Miss Farraday, if she'd mind demonstrating Sasha's solo. "Notice how Miss Farraday stretches her knees tight and keeps everything stiff and pointed. No curves at all."

I sat and stared. Miss Farraday was incredible. It was obvious she used to be a professional dancer, because she was so supple and so controlled. She looked exactly like a mechanical doll dancing, and I wished more than ever that I'd been chosen for this solo.

Everyone applauded loudly when Miss Farraday had finished. Then Don asked the second cast to dance the scene. "Just do the best you can, Tamsyn. I know Miss Farraday is a tough act to follow!"

Tamsyn tossed her head and stuck her chin in the air as she went to take her place. She's such a show-off. I watched her carefully and had to admit she *was* very good, except that Miss Porter had to tap her foot and jab the air with her hand to try and keep Tamsyn on the beat.

"Well done," said Don at the end of the second cast's run-through. He whispered something to Miss Farraday and Miss Porter, then spoke carefully to all of us.

"The mechanical-doll sequence that Miss Farraday demonstrated is extremely difficult. Sasha and Tamsyn have had a good stab at it. But we'd just like to try one or two other people to see if it comes more naturally to anyone else..." Don paused and his eyes scanned us all.

Choose me. Please choose me.

"Amelia, let's start with you."

Amelia walked to the starting place, smiling around at everyone like a queen as she got into position. My heart was beating faster than usual because I was so desperate to be chosen for the part. I looked around and saw several people sitting up straight as sticks. Not Tamsyn though. She had gone back to her seat and was hunched up with folded arms.

"And *three* and *four* and..." said Don.

Off went Amelia, dancing with the most amazing technique. The only trouble was, it was too graceful and flowing and not at all like a clockwork doll. I think Miss Coralie would have said that she wasn't springy and sharp enough.

Don had a quick whispered conference with Miss Porter and Miss Farraday, then said, "Thank you, Amelia." He smiled at her as she went off to the side, but her eyes just clouded over with anger.

I happened to look at Poppy at that moment. She was wildly signaling to me, jerking her head at Don as if to say, "Why don't you ask if *you* can try?" And when I looked at Jazz, I saw that she was doing exactly the same thing. But then I noticed Amelia urgently shaking her head at me. Was she warning me not to put myself forward because it would look like I was showing off and trying to steal the part? But I desperately wanted the chance to show that I could do it.

On the other hand I didn't want to risk annoying the adults, and no one else was volunteering so it obviously wasn't the done thing. I just sat staring at my hands in my lap, not knowing what to do. Then Don cleared his throat, looked at his watch and announced that it was getting short of time so he'd decided to re-choreograph that section to make it simpler. He added that he was sorry, and that it was his own fault for making the steps too difficult, but he didn't want a single step in the ballet that couldn't be carried out absolutely perfectly.

It felt as though the sun had moved behind a big, black cloud. I was so disappointed not to have been asked to try for the solo, as I was certain I could have done it. But, still, I supposed I should have been grateful to Amelia for warning me just in time.

3 Jasmine

"That looks wonderful, Jasmine!" said my mom as I placed the glittery gold star on the very top of the Christmas tree.

I stood back to admire my handiwork, and then imagined how much better the tree would look when all the presents were piled underneath it. There was exactly one week to go till Christmas Day, and I couldn't resist throwing another piece of tinsel over the sparkling branches as a shiver of Christmas magic ran over me.

"Papa will be impressed when he gets back from the gym, won't he?" My mom is French, so I've always called my parents Maman and Papa.

Maman nodded and smiled, and then a wonderful idea popped into my head for no reason at all except general excitement. "Can I call Miss Coralie? I want to tell her how we're doing."

"Well…" I knew Maman was only hesitating because she thinks people shouldn't be disturbed on Sundays.

"I'm sure she'd love to know…"

"Oh, go on then."

I leaped over to the phone before she could change her mind, and my heart started beating loudly at the thought of hearing Miss Coralie's voice. But then I got a surprise because it was a man who answered. I didn't even know Miss Coralie was married.

"Ah, I'm sorry to disturb you, but could I speak to Miss Coralie, please. It's Jasmine Ayed."

There was a pause and then the man spoke in a really grave voice. "I'm afraid Miss Coralie has had to go to hospital."

My hand shot to my mouth and I forgot to speak for a moment I was so shocked. "Oh...oh dear..." I didn't know what to say so I looked at Maman who raised her eyebrows. "Miss Coralie's in hospital," I mouthed helplessly. And then, thank goodness, Maman took the phone from me and I listened while she made sympathetic noises, then asked if she could do anything to help.

"What's the matter with her?" I asked, the second Maman put the phone down.

"I'm afraid poor Miss Coralie's got pneumonia, *chérie*."

"She will be all right, won't she?"

Maman didn't answer immediately and at the time I thought it was because she was still in a kind of a daze with the shock of the news, but when I was lying in bed that night, I looked back at that little pause before Maman had said, "I'm sure she'll be fine," and couldn't help worrying about it. Maybe Maman had used the pause to decide whether or not to tell me a lie, just to make me feel better. Maybe she secretly thought that Miss Coralie wasn't going to be fine at all, because when I'd asked her what pneumonia was, she'd hadn't really answered me, just said that it affected everyone differently and then repeated that Miss Coralie would definitely be fine, and was sure to be better by Christmas.

It took me forever to get to sleep because I'd decided not to tell Rose or Poppy about Miss Coralie being in hospital, in case they started worrying and it affected their dancing. Maman had said that that was very thoughtful and mature of me, and told me she was proud of me, and then she'd quickly added that, of course, there was nothing to worry about really. I don't like keeping secrets from my best friends, but this was important, so I lay there in the dark and made a little promise to myself.

I won't breathe a word about Miss Coralie being sick until I know she's getting better.

I'd been dreading the journey up to London the next day in case Rose and Poppy noticed that I was being too quiet or anything, but as it happened we spent the whole time playing twenty questions about what we'd bought different members of our families for Christmas, because we'd all been Christmas shopping on Sunday morning. Then Poppy made Rose and me laugh, telling us a story about her little brother Stevie.

"He went carol singing with his friend's family and they turned up at our house. It was so funny because when we opened the door there was Stevie wearing reindeer antlers with bells on them. He was trying really hard to make the antlers ring by shaking his head, but he was shaking them so hard that his voice came out all trembly like an opera singer's!"

When we'd finished laughing, Poppy went on, "It feels funny missing out on things like carol singing because of rehearsals, doesn't it?"

I knew what she meant. It *was* sort of weird. But I didn't mind. The *Nutcracker* has always been such a big part of Christmas for us. The three of us have all seen it performed at least three times before, and millions of times on DVD, and now that we're actually dancing in it with people paying to come and see us, it makes Christmas more special than ever.

In the changing room, everyone seemed to be full of Christmas sparkle because there was so much excited chatter and laughter as we got ready. Sue had to keep on telling us to quiet down and you could tell she was getting a little frazzled. A girl called Lizzie was showing us all a routine that she'd learned in her tap classes, which she did amazingly even without tap shoes on. Everyone clapped like crazy, except Amelia who just looked down her nose. I guess she was jealous because she'd never be able to do anything like that herself.

Poppy, Rose and I went to the bathroom afterward, and I decided to mention something that had been on my mind a lot since the last rehearsal.

"You know the steps that Don asked Amelia to try out..."

Rose immediately put her hands on her hips in typical Rose fashion. "You two already talked to me about that on the way home, and I've told you I'm not taking any chances."

"But Rose," I insisted, "you'd be perfect as a mechanical doll. You're so flexible and agile and small."

"Amelia says—"

"Amelia's just jealous," I interrupted. "You saw what she was like with Lizzie just then. She has to have all the attention for herself. And anyway, I've been thinking about when Don was trying people out. I'm sure I saw his eyes on you, but you were looking down and I think he thought that meant you didn't want to give it a try."

"Well, that's ridiculous, because if ever I look down at school, I *still* get picked!"

"Yes, but I think it's different with an important show like this," said Poppy. "Don can't risk choosing people who don't seem confident enough, because they might not put everything into it."

"And that's no good for a performance," I finished off.

Rose's eyes widened, then she made a face. "How come I always get everything wrong? I'm either showing off too much or trying so hard *not* to show off that I'm making people think I'm not interested. It's so unfair."

"It's a shame because that part of the ballet's not half as good with the changed choreography," said Poppy thoughtfully. Then she frowned. "But I think it's too late to say anything now. It would be awful if Don and Mr. Rivas and everyone thought you were being...pushy, Rose."

Rose sighed. "Yeah, you're right, Poppy." Then she turned to me. "Amelia *does* know what she's talking about, Jazz. I mean, if I suddenly asked to try out the steps, Don would think I was the biggest show-off under the sun. And anyway, he's decided against it now, so he won't want to waste time going back to it..." Then Rose suddenly cracked up laughing. "Isn't this conversation the wrong way around?" she spluttered. "Aren't *you* supposed to be the sensible one, Jazz, and I'm the one who usually opens my big mouth and puts my foot in it!"

I couldn't help laughing too, but then I thought about Amelia again, and knew I just didn't trust her. "I honestly think that Amelia's a selfish person, Rose," I said carefully. "I think that all she cares about is making sure that *you*

can't have something she can't have herself."
Rose looked thoughtful so I decided to continue.
"What if you just wait till we're rehearsing the
part where Don wanted to have the doll solo,
then say in your politest voice, 'Excuse me, but
could I possibly show you the other
choreography, Don, because I've been practicing
and I'm sure I can do it.' That's not showing off.
It's being helpful and mature. Plus, Don will be
impressed that you've been practicing."

Rose was wearing a heavy frown by now and I
was desperately trying to think of a way to make
her see that I was right, when suddenly I got it.

"Miss Coralie would be really proud of you,
you know." I'd been really careful not to show
any sadness in my voice because of what I knew
about Miss Coralie being in hospital, but Rose
and Poppy were looking at me very intently, and
I thought I must have given something away
after all. Then I realized they were just thinking
hard about Miss Coralie.

"It feels weird sometimes, not having her teaching us, doesn't it?" said Rose.

I knew what she meant. "Yes, once or twice during warm-up I've realized that I've had a slightly bent supporting leg or something, and that Miss Farraday hasn't spotted it and I've thought of Miss Coralie and made myself try harder. I mean, I know it's only a warm-up, not a real class, but all the same..."

"Miss Coralie would be just as strict for warm-up as for class, wouldn't she?" Poppy said. "Because she wouldn't want anyone to drop their standards even for a second."

Rose nodded, then said she was going back to the changing room because she wanted to put more hairpins in her hair. I decided not to say any more about her asking Don if she could try out the mechanical doll steps. I just hoped she'd think about what I'd said about Miss Coralie. Poppy went off with Rose but I stayed behind to wash my hands, which I'd just seen had got some dried glue on them from where I'd been making Christmas cards the day before.

I couldn't stop thinking about the doll solo and feeling disappointed that Rose hadn't been asked. Then I started imagining doing it *myself*. I stood in front of the full-length mirror beside the door and concentrated on looking like a mechanical doll. I opened my eyes as wide as they'd go, and sucked in my cheeks until I was going cross-eyed and my bottom lip had practically disappeared. I knew I looked funny, but I didn't care because no one was there to see me. Finally I locked my knees right back and raised my arms with sharp angles at the elbows and stiff hands nearly touching in front. And that was when one of the dancers from the company came in and looked at me with laughter in her eyes, before disappearing into one of the stalls.

Oh no! She must think I'm a complete idiot, I said to myself as I scuttled back to the changing room. I bet she'll go and spread it to the other dancers in the company that one of the students is crazy, then she'll point me out and they'll all stare at me during rehearsals. It will be so embarrassing.

"Good, we're all here," said Sue, the moment I walked in. "Ready to go through to the studio, girls? Remember, you're rehearsing with the dancers from the company today, and you students will be expected to be as quiet as little mice, so they don't even notice you when you're not actually involved."

I saw Amelia and Tamsyn exchange a look. I know Sue speaks to us as though we're much younger than we are, but that's because she's an old-fashioned type of person. I don't mind at all. At least she's nice, and that's all that matters. But as we walked down the hallway, Amelia and Tamsyn were whispering together behind their hands.

"I bet they're saying nasty things about Sue," said Rose.

I nodded, but I was thinking that actually they could have been saying nasty things about *anyone*. They're both attention seekers and show-offs, and who knew what they would get up to now they'd gotten together.

Inside the studio, I felt a thrill at the sight of all the professional dancers. Some of them were stretching and limbering in the center, and others were marking steps with Don and Mr. Rivas. They were all totally focused and didn't take any notice of us at all. So it gave me a shock when Amelia went right up to one of them and said, "Hi, Carly! Remember me? Amelia Kent?"

The dancer blinked a little then said, "Oh yes... Hi."

"So, what role have you got this year?" went on Amelia quite loudly (to make sure we all heard, I suppose).

"Er...I'm the Sugarplum Fairy."

"Oh, great!" said Amelia. "I love that music."

Then Miss Farraday asked us each to find a place on the *barre,* and we started the warm-up. I found it hard to concentrate because all I wanted to do was stare at the dancers. I managed to sneak one or two glances though, and noticed that most of the girls were wearing vest tops and tights with leg warmers. Some wore ballet skirts too, which came down below their knees. This was probably to try and get the feel of what it would be like dancing in their costumes. The men all wore tights or sweatpants with vest tops or T-shirts.

I was sure I'd spotted the dancer who had the role of Clara because she was the tiniest. In fact, she was only the same height as Poppy. She was wearing a floaty tulle skirt. It was fairly tatty, and I guessed it was an old one left over from another performance. Her *pointe* shoes looked sort of worn too. But her hair was scraped back neatly and twizzled around into a bun.

We'd hardly finished the first exercise when

Miss Farraday suddenly clapped her hands and said, "I know you're all fascinated by the presence of the company dancers, but I need you to concentrate hard, so no more wandering eyes, thank you very much."

In the end she gave up. I could tell by her pursed lips that she wasn't very happy. "We may as well get on with rehearsal. Don..."

And that was when I suddenly spotted the dancer who'd come into the bathroom and seen me doing that embarrassing doll imitation. I quickly looked away and hoped that she'd forgotten about me by now.

Don didn't need to raise his voice at all. "First cast, in positions please. Second-cast students, ready to watch carefully."

Lizzie and I went over to take our places in front of the two dancers who were playing the roles of our mother and father. Once Andy had started to play the piano I concentrated hard on listening for our cue, then in no time at all we were dancing the steps we'd rehearsed so much. It was magic.

When both casts had practiced the scene for nearly two hours, Don said the students could take a break while he worked on a particular part with Lisette Canning, the girl who was dancing the part of Clara. So everyone headed for the door. But Poppy and I hung back so we could keep watching Lisette for a few more seconds. I'd thought we were the last to go, but it turned out that I was wrong because I suddenly spotted Rose standing right next to Don.

My heart raced at the sound of her voice. "'Scuse me, Don, but..."

Poppy shot me a glance with big scared eyes. We were obviously both thinking the same thing. Rose must have decided she was going to ask Don about the mechanical doll solo, but she'd chosen completely the wrong moment.

Don frowned hard. You could tell he was annoyed. "Is it important?"

Rose hesitated and I prayed that she'd say no, but she didn't. "I just wanted to show you something."

"It'll have to wait, I'm afraid," came the snappy reply, then Don turned to Lisette. "You can use more space in the opening, Lisette... Andy, can we take it from the top of that section?"

And Rose was forgotten. She rushed over to me and Poppy, looking really upset. "See! I knew I shouldn't have said anything."

"It's just that Don was really busy at that moment, Rose," I whispered back.

But Rose interrupted in a hiss. "There wasn't any other chance, was there? And it was *you* who insisted I had to say something today. Now he thinks I'm stupid and rude."

Poppy put her arm around Rose. "I'm sure there'll be a chance next time. And once Don sees how good you are, he'll completely forget about today."

Rose didn't reply, just marched out to catch up with the line of students going to the canteen. I sighed and felt miserable. She was obviously angry with me. Poppy hurried after her, but I couldn't resist lingering at the door for a moment longer to watch Lisette working with Don, even though I could hear Sue down the hallway telling the stragglers to hurry up.

I wish I *had* hurried up now, because I suddenly realized that the dancer I'd seen in the bathroom was looking right at me and whispering to one of the other dancers. Then the other dancer looked over in my direction too and I saw that they were both trying to hide their grins, so I quickly pulled the door shut and hurried down the hallway with a very hot face, wishing I could start this day all over again.

4 Poppy

Today we all had costume fittings. It was so exciting. My costume for the Christmas party scene fits perfectly and doesn't need a single alteration. It's a beautiful shade of blue called midnight blue and it goes right in at the waist, then flares out from my hips. The sleeves are lacy and go down to my elbows, and I have to wear a thin gold tiara on my head. Bettina, who is the wardrobe mistress, made me dance a few steps so she could make sure that I felt completely comfortable wearing the tiara. "We don't want it to inhibit your movements," she said, staring at me with knitted eyebrows as I tried to dance, feeling rather stupid dancing all on my own in front of Bettina. She's kind of a scary person and doesn't say much at all. So it was a lovely surprise when she suddenly gave me a half smile. "That blue goes beautifully with your auburn hair, Poppy."

When I told Jasmine and Rose what she'd said, in the changing room afterward, Amelia must have overheard.

"Bettina always compliments everyone," she said in her loud voice. "Last year she told me I had a perfect dancer's body and that I'd even look nice dressed in a black bin liner!"

All the joy that I'd felt at Bettina's words fizzled away when Amelia said that, but then it came back when Lizzie spoke.

"Well, it's not true that she compliments everyone, actually, because she asked me if I was suffering from wrigglitis and said I'd have to learn to stand still if I didn't want her to glue my feet to the floor."

Everyone laughed and Lizzie rolled her eyes.

"I thought she was really scary," said Jasmine. "She hardly spoke a word to me, just nodded when she'd finished."

"Me too," said Rose.

"Well, I had to spend a long time standing around with hardly any clothes on while she fiddled with my headdress," said Sasha. "I was freezing."

"You should have asked her if she was going to visit you in hospital when you caught pneumonia!" said Lizzie, which set us all off snickering again. Well, all except Jasmine. I noticed she looked as though she was about to burst into tears and I wondered what on earth could be the matter, so as soon as everyone had gone back to their own conversations, I asked her if she was okay.

She immediately broke into a big grin and said, "Yes, I'm fine. Totally fine."

But I didn't believe her. She was smiling too

brightly when she'd just been so upset. And the smile wasn't real. Her eyes were still sad.

"I can't wait till we have the dress rehearsal," she went on.

"I can't either," I said, picturing Jasmine in her beautiful ivory party dress with the silver sash, and Rose in her dark-green silky dress with the golden sash.

"I bet the Christmas party scene will look like a grand glittering ball!" said Rose.

I agreed with her. My favorite part of the whole *Nutcracker* ballet is the Christmas party. It's wonderful dancing with a ballerina like Lisette Canning. And there's one magical moment when Lisette and I have to do two *jetés* at exactly the same time, then lean our heads close together, because in the story I'm supposed to be her friend. She always smiles at me and I smile back, and I've often wished that Jasmine or Rose could quickly take a photo of that moment so I could keep it forever. But, of course, there's no way that could ever happen.

Today is the twentieth of December and we're going to be rehearsing *Waltz of the Flowers* with the professional dancers for the first time and I'm a complete nervous wreck. You see, I just don't seem to be able to do this dance right and I can't figure out why, when I love the music so much, and Rose and Jasmine and I are always dancing it at home. I keep worrying that I'm not good enough, and the only thing that makes me feel better is remembering something that Tamsyn said. She was boasting about how she's just as talented as Amelia. "I feel so honored to have been picked to dance the same role as Amelia, because it's obvious all the adults think she's the best, otherwise why did she get through the auditions two years running? So that means they must think I'm up to the same standard as Amelia."

I remember how Rose's lip curled when Tamsyn said that, and I knew she was thinking what a show-off Tamsyn was. And it was true, she was. But the reason her words cheer me up when I feel nervous is because for the Christmas party scene, *I've* got the same part as Amelia, just like Tamsyn has in Act Two. So does that mean *I'm* as good as Amelia, too? If only I was in the same cast as Jasmine and Rose, I wouldn't be worrying about these things because they wouldn't let me.

Right now, Tamsyn and Amelia are standing up very straight right in the middle of the studio, with their feet turned out in first position. They're talking to each other using their hands in a graceful but over-the-top way, and it's obvious they're trying to get noticed. I looked around for Jasmine and Rose. They were right at the back of the studio in a corner. Poor Rose felt really stiff this morning and she obviously still wasn't right because she was sitting in the sideways splits, leaning her top half flat on the ground to try and loosen up her hips and the tops of her legs.

"Wow! Someone's very flexible!" said the dancer called Carly, who's got the role of the Sugarplum Fairy.

Immediately Rose jumped up and stood as still as a statue. The trouble is, she's scared stiff that people will think she's showing off.

Amelia and Tamsyn were looking absolutely furious. "I think it's time that girl was taught a lesson," I heard Amelia say in a low voice, before she and Tamysn went off to the side whispering to each other.

All the company dancers are very nice and always smile at us but hardly ever say anything, and we were told by Sue that we weren't to talk to them unless they talked to us first. If any of them does happen to say a few words, we gather around like lots of little birds hoping to be thrown some more crumbs. Today, it was Rose who'd been the lucky one, not that *she* would think so.

"Okay, let's start with the second cast for a change," said Don.

In a flash, Tamsyn was on her feet, running over to her starting place. Then, when we were all in position, Don signaled to Andy and the music began. I danced with as much expression as I possibly could, but as usual I wasn't filled with tingles like I am at home, and I knew it wasn't my best, which made me feel anxious again.

"Stretch up, Poppy," said Don. "That's right...and you can do a bigger scoop with your arms just before you turn for the *pas de bourrée*."

Afterward, I felt angry with myself for being the only one to get corrected and sat with my knees up to my chin and my arms wrapped around them, ready to watch the first cast. There were a few moments with nothing happening except Don and Mr. Rivas talking together, their backs to us, and Andy running through pieces of his music while everyone else stayed in their own little worlds, marking things out. But then Mr. Rivas suddenly turned around and ran his eyes over the second cast and, horror of horrors, they settled on me. The moment he saw that I happened to be looking right back at him, he quickly turned away again and kept on talking to Don.

My heart started thumping, I was so scared that they might be saying my dancing wasn't good enough. What if they decided to replace me with one of the reserves? If that happened I wouldn't be able to bear it. It would be the very worst thing that had ever *ever* happened in my whole life.

I hated these thoughts. They were making me so nervous and uncomfortable. I tried to shake them away because I needed to feel right, or my dancing would be even worse. Then I started hoping that the rehearsal would end for lunch soon, so that I could talk to Jasmine and Rose. I sighed a big sigh as my eyes traveled over to Rose. Everyone in her cast was in position now, ready to start rehearsing. Rose herself was standing perfectly still, staring right ahead. Amelia was trying to attract her attention, but Rose was just ignoring her, thank goodness. I was sure Amelia was trying to distract Rose to get her into trouble. She and Tamsyn were exchanging looks and they were definitely up to something.

I looked at Jasmine standing next to Lizzie and saw that she was staring into the distance too. It was difficult to tell from across the studio but it looked as though she had tears in her eyes. Poor Jazz. I couldn't understand what on earth could be making her sad, but stranger still was why she was keeping it to herself. I thought we three shared all our secrets.

A moment later, Don was ready for the first cast to start and immediately a hush fell over the studio. As they went through the dance, I lost myself in a lovely dream about Lisette Canning and me becoming friends in real life, because the day before she'd asked me where I lived and said she loved that part of the world. But my dream kept being interrupted by horrible nagging worries that I might be thrown out of the *Nutcracker* for not being good enough. Each time I got myself into a bad mood thinking about that, I quickly reminded myself that for the Christmas Party scene Amelia and I are both dancing the same roles. So surely I should feel proud of myself, just as Tamsyn said she felt honored for having the same role as Amelia in *Waltz of the Flowers.* The only trouble was, I didn't really believe I was anywhere near as good as Amelia and I felt sure there must be another reason why we'd both been chosen for the same role.

All these thoughts were racing around inside my head and it suddenly felt as though I couldn't bear them for a second longer, so I leaned forward to Tamsyn, who was sitting just in front of me.

"We're lucky, aren't we?" I blurted out. "Because I have the same role as Amelia in Act One, and *you're* her opposite in Act Two."

But the moment the words were out of my mouth, I thought how babyish and pathetic they sounded, especially when Tamsyn turned around with a big sneer on her face. "Act One isn't as important as Act Two, actually. I think the only reason they chose you for that role is because of the part where your head has to go close to Lisette's. I mean, no one else is as tall as her, are they? And they probably only chose Amelia from the other cast because she's the second tallest."

My heart seemed to be beating near my throat now. This wasn't what I wanted to hear. I wished I'd never spoken, then at least I could have kept on dreaming that I was as good as Amelia.

I was really upset then and Don was calling us back to have another run-through. This was going to be so bad. My whole body was trembling. I nearly told Sue I wasn't feeling well, but I couldn't do that. I just had to get on with it.

We were on the point of starting when the studio door opened and Lisette put her head around and quickly scanned the room, obviously looking for someone. She didn't find them, but along the way her eyes met mine and she gave me a quick smile before disappearing.

I clung like crazy to the memory of that smile for the whole rest of the rehearsal. And I think it was the only thing that made my dancing okay.

Not brilliant though. No, definitely not brilliant.

5 Rose

I'm doing a countdown. It's the twenty-first of December and we've just arrived at the studios for rehearsal. Three days to go till the first performance on Christmas Eve! It's so weird feeling more excited about Christmas Eve than Christmas Day this year.

The moment Poppy, Jazz and I went into the changing room, Amelia pounced on me.

"Hi, Rose!"

I didn't really feel like talking, but I was trying to make a big effort to be as friendly as possible toward Amelia whenever we weren't actually in the studio, so that she might leave me alone during rehearsals. You see, I'm getting tired of the number of times she talks to me when I'm trying to concentrate. It's all right for her. Everyone thinks she's great. She doesn't have to prove herself at all because all the artistic staff know her from last year. But every time she talks to me I worry that I'll be the one who will get in trouble for not concentrating.

I've got sort of a bad reputation when it comes to focusing. In fact, I got in terrible trouble for playing around with Kieran when he first joined Miss Coralie's, and I nearly lost the chance of taking my grade four exam. But now it's extra important that I don't let my concentration slip. I can't risk getting told off, especially after Don was so annoyed with me when I tried to ask him if I could show him the mechanical-doll solo.

"What do you think of this, Rose?" Amelia was peeling the waistband on her tights down, and there on the very bottom of her back was a tattoo of a nutcracker. It was wicked.

"Wow! It's not real though, is it?"

"Yeah!" Her big blue eyes were wide open, all innocent and shocked. But I still didn't believe her.

"Your parents would never let you have a real tattoo."

"They would, actually. My mom's got one herself – on her shoulder."

I looked more closely at the nutcracker. It certainly did look real. "It's good, isn't it, Rose?" said a girl called Laura. Then everyone was flocking around, giving Amelia big compliments about how cool she is.

Amelia seemed very interested in my opinion all of a sudden. "Anyway, do you like it, Rose?"

"Yeah, it's okay."

"Well, look!" She rushed over to where her jeans were on the bench and pulled a packet of fake tattoos out of her pocket. "I bought these just after I'd had mine done. They actually sold them at the front of the tattoo shop. They're fake but they last forever. Why don't you have one? Look, you can have any of these Christmas designs. What about this Rudolph the Red-nosed Reindeer? That'd be good."

"Hey, can I have one, Amelia?" asked Tamsyn.

"Can *I*?" asked Sasha.

Then lots of people asked.

"No," said Amelia. "I'm saving them. Except for one for Rose and one for Tamsyn," she added.

I saw a look pass between Amelia and Tamsyn but I wasn't sure what it meant. I knew Amelia was very friendly with Tamsyn, but why had she chosen *me*? I didn't get it.

"Go on, Rose. Take your pick. You can have any one you want."

"I don't think so."

She thrust the Rudolph tattoo under my nose.

"Why don't you take this one?"

In the end I agreed because it was the best way to shut her up. "How long does it last for?"

"A week? Longer if you don't wash. Here, I'll put it on for you. Where do you want it?"

"Don't have it where it'll show, Rose," Jazz said quietly and I shot her a grateful look because I hadn't even thought of that.

"Same place as yours, I suppose," I said.

So Amelia stuck it on, only it didn't feel as low as hers. In fact, it was just on the back of my waist.

"Don't pull your tights up completely for a minute, Rose," Jazz said. "It might mark them."

Then Amelia stuck a Christmas star tattoo on the bottom of Tamsyn's back, only hers seemed much lower down than mine.

"It only takes a few seconds to dry, doesn't it?" said Tamsyn. "Then it'll be fine, won't it?"

But Amelia didn't reply, just went over to her ballet bag and quickly dropped the tattoos in there because Sue had come in to the changing room.

"Two minutes, then we're off, girls," she said, looking around to make sure that we all looked presentable.

I couldn't help feeling guilty. Somehow, I didn't think Sue would approve if she knew about our fake tattoos. Never mind, I could wash mine off as soon as I got home.

The rehearsal went really well that day. I was filled with major jitters because we were getting so much nearer to the first performance now. But they weren't the nasty, school exam sort of jitters; they were the brilliant, buzzy ones that make you want to fly.

During lunch I was called to go for a costume fitting. My costume had needed an alteration, so I had to go back to make sure it was all right now. If only Bettina wasn't such a scary person. Poppy was the only one who'd managed to get a smile and a compliment out of her. Well,

Amelia *said* she'd got a big compliment about her lovely figure last year, but personally I don't believe her. I think it was just Amelia showing off again.

Sue had already explained to us how precious the costumes are because each and every one is handmade. She'd also said we must never eat or drink while wearing our costumes, and we have to try not to sit down either, especially if we're wearing one of the beautiful tulle skirts that look like long floaty tutus. So, when Bettina was sliding the costume over my head I felt as though I couldn't move a muscle. I was very glad I was facing her because I'd suddenly remembered about my tattoo, and didn't want her to notice it. I could imagine her going crazy and sticking pins in me if she caught sight of Rudolph's red nose. So I made sure I stood as still as a statue while she fiddled with my costume, even though I really wanted to spin around and make the silky green material of the skirt fly out in swishy swirls. When she'd finished adjusting my waistband she stood back. "Right, hop up on the step; let's have a good look."

I did as I was told, then had to turn around very slowly with my arms out to the sides.

"All right, you'll do."

And the next minute she was easing the costume up over my head and telling me to put my leotard back on.

"What's this?"

I looked up quickly. She was pointing to a red mark on the costume.

"How did that get there? Hmm?"

I gulped.

"You're looking very guilty, young lady. Let's have a look at your back."

So I had to show her.

"Stupid girl!" she said in a very angry voice. Then she shook her head and kept staring at the costume as though she couldn't believe how anyone could be so idiotic as to have stuck a tattoo on their back. "Have you any idea how delicate this material is?"

"Sorry," I mumbled. "I didn't realize…"

Then she shook her head some more and talked about wasting time before picking up a notebook.

"There, I've made a note to report it. Your chaperone will be making sure there's not a single trace of it tomorrow. Now, off you go."

I mumbled another "sorry", finished getting dressed, then made a run for it, feeling very stupid and alarmed. What did Bettina mean by "I've made a note to report it"? Who was she going to report it *to*? My heart was beating really fast as I went back to the studios, in case she meant Mr. Rivas. Then I remembered the look that had passed between Amelia and Tamsyn. Did they know I'd get into trouble? Did they plan the whole thing? And what about Tamsyn? She went for a fitting earlier. Did she get a telling-off too?

That afternoon we rehearsed the Christmas

party scene again. I didn't say a word to Tamsyn or Amelia about what Bettina had said. In fact, I didn't say a word to them about anything. I simply didn't talk to them because I was so annoyed. They *must* have known I'd get into trouble for having a tattoo.

Don wasn't there today, but when we got to the part where he'd had to change the choreography, I felt more frustrated than ever that I hadn't had the chance to show him what I could do. The ballet just wasn't the same with the new choreography. It took all my powers of concentration to ignore these angry feelings and get on with my part.

There's a time near the end of the scene, where Amelia and I have to pretend to have a secret. We usually smile at each other like best friends, but there was no way I could bring myself to do it today, and Miss Farraday got annoyed, which made me feel even worse than I did already.

"Rose and Amelia, in ballet, and indeed in

drama, if you have to smile at your deadliest enemy, you do so. Understand?"

I stood stiffly and nodded.

Amelia said, "Sorry, Miss Farraday." Then she jerked her head at me, turned her palms up and lifted her shoulders as if to say, *It's Rose's fault, not mine.*

I opened my mouth to protest but then realized that actually it was true. It *was* my fault. I was the one who couldn't bring myself to smile at Amelia, so unless I explained everything about the tattoo, which would take forever and probably put Miss Farraday in even more of a bad mood, I just had to put up with taking the blame. And that made me even madder. But it also scared me to death. I did a little add-up of the trouble I'd been in since starting the *Nutcracker* rehearsals. I'd managed to make Bettina angry (with a big risk of Mr. Rivas and Sue being even madder), I'd annoyed Miss Farraday by not smiling when I was supposed to and I'd got on Don's nerves by butting in when he was far too busy to listen to a silly little student like me. So I knew that from now on I definitely mustn't put a foot wrong because I could easily be thrown out – that's if they hadn't decided to throw me out already. I shivered and squeezed my eyes tight shut to blot out that terrible thought. I had to get focused again because it was time for *Waltz of the Flowers*.

When I watched the second cast dancing it, I thought Poppy looked as though there was something the matter with her too. She seemed to be struggling to make the steps flow. I noticed that Mr. Rivas took her to one side at the end, and whatever he said made Poppy turn pink and look flustered, but he patted her on the shoulder before she came over to join us.

Then Miss Farraday had a word with all the *Waltz of the Flowers* students. "I think you girls have worked hard enough for today, so you're free to go along to the lunchroom if you want until your parents come to collect you. Amelia, can you go along to wardrobe please... And I'll see you all tomorrow. Don't forget we're rehearsing at the theater tomorrow, which will be hard work but should also be very exciting as you're going to be dancing on the actual stage where you'll be performing. Now, get a good night's sleep, everyone."

The company dancers clapped as we left the room. They always clap at the end of rehearsals to say thank you to the people who have been taking the rehearsal, but it was nice that they clapped for us too. Then Sue took us down to the lunchroom and said she'd be back when the others had finished.

There were several people in the lunchroom who worked for *Ballet Theater UK* but weren't dancers or artistic staff, and it reminded me of what a big company it is, with so many office people. I said to Jazz that I'd grab us a table if she wanted to get the drinks.

"Okay, you two go and save me a place."

I was just sitting down when Poppy gasped. "Look what she's wearing! It's not allowed in the lunchroom!"

I didn't know what she was talking about at first, but when I looked up I got a big shock. Amelia was standing at Tamsyn's table all dressed up in her costume.

I heard Sasha say, "You look beautiful, Amelia!" And next minute, Amelia was smiling like a queen as she looked over to our table to make sure that we were equally impressed.

"You shouldn't be wearing that in here!" I called out to her. "What are you doing?"

Her eyes went from superior to snappy in a flash. "Bettina hasn't even noticed I've left, she's so busy with one of the dancers. But even if she does, she'd never be angry with me. I'd just say I had to go to the bathroom." She tossed her head as she strutted over to us and calmly pulled out a chair at our table because there were no spaces at Tamsyn's. "Have you seen all these sequins? Bettina says I've got the most!"

"We're saving that seat for Jazz, actually," said Poppy.

Amelia looked annoyed. "I'm only staying for a few minutes. I'm sure *Jazz* can find someone else to sit with."

That made me mad. "We want her here, actually. And anyway, you're not allowed to sit down with your costume on."

"Yes, remember what Sue said," Poppy added, looking anxiously at Amelia's costume. "You'll spoil the tulle."

Amelia rolled her eyes. "Honestly, you two, you follow all the rules like little kids. I was here last year, remember, so I do know what I'm doing. They only get the chaperones to give us the lecture about how precious the costumes are for the benefit of boys and clumsy people. *I'm* not going to get this messed up, am I? I'm being really careful."

I glanced up and saw that Jazz was on her way back with the drinks and three bananas. "Right, you'll have to go now, Amelia." Then I couldn't help what I said next because I reckoned it was about time someone put that girl in her place. "Why not go and show your wonderful sequins to someone else?"

I wasn't prepared for what happened next. *Nobody* was. Amelia gave me a daggers look and swung around in a big temper, knocking into the tray Jazz was carrying, and making one of the mugs of cocoa wobble dangerously.

I leaped up to grab it, but it was too late. It tipped over. The tray was instantly awash with brown liquid, the floor was speckled and spotted, Jazz had drips and splashes on her top, but worst of all, the whole of the front of Amelia's white costume was spattered with tiny brown marks.

We all stared in horror.

6 Jasmine

My heart stopped beating, and my arms were trembling so much I could hardly manage to keep hold of the tray I was carrying.

"Quick! Cloth!" I managed to squeak.

And Rose shot over to the counter. The serving lady had seen what had happened and was already on her way.

"Put it down, dear," she said calmly to me.

So I did, and she immediately started wiping up the cocoa that had slopped in the tray.

"What about my dress!" wailed Amelia, her cheeks flooding with color.

"Oh, dear dear dear!" said the lady. She shook her head and did a lot of tutting. "You're going to have to get back to wardrobe, young lady." She pointed at Amelia's costume, doing little jabs in the air. "And I wouldn't like to be you when the wardrobe mistress sees the state of that. There's a reason for rules, you know." Then she went off with the half-empty mug. "I'll get another hot chocolate."

Amelia turned to me with a look of hate in her eyes. "Thanks *very* much, Jasmine Ayed." And she marched off, leaving me feeling sick with worry.

"It wasn't Jazz's fault," Rose called out angrily.

Amelia mumbled something in reply, but I could only make out the word "clumsy" before she was out of the door.

By this time, the whole lunchroom was quiet – all the office staff were watching us curiously, and there were some dancers looking in our direction too. My heart banged. One of them was the dancer who'd caught me pretending to be a mechanical doll in the bathroom. She wasn't smiling now. In fact she looked deadly serious. Now she must think I was stupid and clumsy, as well as weird.

The other *Waltz of the Flowers* students were whispering to each other at their table on the other side of the room.

"It *wasn't* your fault," repeated Poppy. "It definitely wasn't."

I didn't say anything, but the thoughts were whizzing around inside my head. Amelia was so popular, she could say whatever she wanted and everyone would believe her. What if I got a big telling-off from Bettina? Or worse still, what if Bettina reported me to Miss Farraday or one of the other teachers? I couldn't bear that.

Rose must have been reading my mind. "Everybody saw what happened, Jazz. No one's going to blame you."

I shivered and thought about the dancer's eyes as she'd stared over at me. Then when I glanced in her direction a moment later I saw that she'd gone. The office staff were back in their conversations and Tamsyn was demonstrating to the other students on her table how double-jointed her shoulders were. I felt completely knotted up inside because now I had to worry about getting into trouble for something that wasn't my fault, as well as feeling sad about Miss Coralie. I didn't know which was worse. I suppose they were just different. One was a huge worry bubbling away, making me tense, and the other was a deep sadness that sat like a stone inside me.

The trouble was, Maman had told me she was going to call Miss Coralie's husband yesterday to find out how she was doing, but when I'd asked her about the phone call in the evening, all she would say was that Miss Coralie was being well looked after in the hospital.

"But is she getting better?" I'd asked, and Maman hadn't answered – well, not really. "She's in the best possible hands to get better, *chérie*." And I just knew she was keeping something from me, and that it must be something really serious.

Then, right in the middle of these sad thoughts, I saw that Poppy was upset about something too. I could see there were tears in her eyes, and immediately forgot about my own sadness.

"What, Poppy?" I asked, putting my arm around her.

And she explained in a shaky voice that she was really worried she wasn't good enough to stay in the *Nutcracker*.

"What rubbish!" said Rose.

"Why are you having these thoughts all of a sudden?" I asked.

"I've had them for a long time, but now they're worse than ever because Tamsyn said I was probably only chosen for the role I've got in the first act because I'm the tallest..." She stopped talking and looked from Rose to me and back again with big frightened eyes. "I'm not *that* tall, am I?"

"No!" said Rose. "Of course you're not!"

"You're perfect," I said. Then I dropped my voice. "And you can't listen to Tamsyn. You know how she has to be the best at everything."

"I bet Tamsyn was worried that you were getting too good and that you might outshine her," Rose added.

"There's no chance of that happening," said Poppy, with a quiver in her voice. "I'm hopeless in the *Waltz of the Flowers*. And I just don't get why, when it's always been my favorite music."

Rose frowned, then after a moment said, "Wait a minute, let's think what Miss Coralie would say to help you..."

And as soon as I heard that name, I felt my throat going tight and knew that tears were coming into my eyes. But I also knew I couldn't let the other two know that I was worried, especially Poppy. She had enough to worry about. If she found out about Miss Coralie she'd be in such a state that she might not be able to dance at all.

"What's the matter, Jasmine?" said Poppy.

Oh no! Think of something. Anything...

"I've just got something in my eye. Ow!" I turned away and pretended to be looking on the table behind for a paper napkin.

The other two were completely quiet and when I turned back Rose said, "Have you got something in *both* eyes, Jazz?"

"Yes...sometimes that happens to me... When one eye starts watering the other one starts too." I was blinking away and my tears were disappearing, thank goodness. So now I just had the lump in my throat to get rid of. That wasn't so easy because I couldn't get the thought of Miss Coralie out of my head.

"Are you okay now, Jasmine?" Poppy asked me quietly.

"Yes, that's better." I nodded and smiled, probably a little too brightly, and kept on talking as though there'd never been anything the matter. "Can't wait for tomorrow! Full rehearsal at the theater!"

"Yesss!" said Poppy and Rose at exactly the same moment.

"And only three days till the first performance!" added Rose. Then she clapped her hand over her mouth. "Sorry, Poppy. I wasn't thinking."

"It's okay," said Poppy. "I've got used to the thought that I won't be dancing with you two on Christmas Eve."

"And when it's your turn in January, *we'll* be finished and you'll be the one having a wonderful time!" I pointed out.

Poppy looked thoughtful. "I wonder if Miss Coralie will come to see the show twice?"

The tears pricked my eyes again and this

time, no matter how hard I blinked, I couldn't stop one from rolling down my cheek.

"It's something about Miss Coralie that's upsetting you, isn't it?" said Poppy, pulling her chair closer and putting her arm around me. "What is it, Jasmine? Please tell us."

And I suppose it was because she was being so kind and sweet that I found myself actually crying then.

Rose reached across the table and gave my hand a squeeze. "What's happened, Jazz? You've got to tell us."

So I had to. I had no choice.

"She's got pneumonia," I said in a small, cracked voice. "She's in the hospital. I didn't want you two to be as upset as me in case it...you know...affected your dancing..."

"Oh no! That's terrible!" said Rose.

"But she will be okay, won't she?" said Poppy.

This time, I knew I had to put on the best act of my life. "Yes, Maman says she'll be all right.

They're...looking after her really well in the hospital..." I was just feeling my voice faltering when a thought popped into my head. "And even though Miss Coralie might not be better in time to see me and Rose dancing, I'm sure she'll be able to come and see you, Poppy."

I managed to give them both shaky smiles and I think I must have made them believe that Miss Coralie was going to be all right, because Poppy looked thoughtful but not too sad, and Rose had a very determined look in her eye that I hadn't been expecting.

"I've been thinking about Miss Coralie, actually," she said.

"What about her?" I asked.

But she never did answer because, at that moment, Amelia suddenly came back in, wearing her own clothes and looking completely normal, as though she didn't have a care in the world. She dragged a chair from another table, squashed it between Tamsyn's and Laura's, and sat down. Sasha and a girl called Jessica were also at the table and they were all watching Amelia with big eyes, probably dying to find out what Bettina had said, like I was.

"Did you get into trouble?" said Tamsyn. "Was Bettina really mad?"

I held my breath and watched Amelia's face carefully. "No," she drawled. "Bettina said it was no problem because it would come off easily." Her eyes flashed over to our table and a haughty sneer came over her face. "I knew she wouldn't be upset." Then she turned a nasty look on me. "Well, not with *me*, anyway."

I gasped.

So did Rose. "You'd better not have said it was Jazz's fault, Amelia Kent! Everyone saw what happened. No one's going to believe you."

I looked around for the secretaries who'd been in earlier but they'd gone now. The only people who'd been here when Amelia had knocked into my tray were the people on Tamsyn's table.

"You saw what happened, didn't you?" said Rose, looking right at Tamsyn.

Tamsyn's eyes flicked over to Amelia. "It was Jasmine's fault," she said with a sly look in her eye. Then she looked at the others on the table. "Wasn't it?"

Amelia was sitting with a look of *just you dare* in her eyes. My heart started to beat. I could see exactly what was happening. Nobody wanted to go against Amelia and Tamsyn because they made such a scary pair. Laura and Jessica lowered their eyes immediately, and Sasha looked as though she might faint or be sick at any second. Nobody said a single word, and a look of triumph came over Amelia's face.

But it soon changed with what Rose said next. "It's strange that Bettina wasn't angry, because when I got a red mark on my costume from that tattoo *you* gave me, Amelia, Bettina was really upset. She said I had to wash the tattoo off by tomorrow, and she's going to report it."

Poppy and I both hid our gasps. You could tell Amelia was taken aback too. Her eyes went big and round and she blinked a few times, but she tried to cover her shock by pulling the hairband off her ponytail, shaking her hair around her shoulders and talking to the other girls at her table as though nothing was the matter and none of that horrible episode had taken place at all.

The three of us leaned forward and began talking quietly again.

"So what do you think Bettina meant about reporting your tattoo, Rose?" asked Poppy.

Rose sighed a huge sigh. "I'm just praying she meant she was going to report it to Sue and not to…Mr. Rivas."

"Well, was it a *really* bad telling off that Bettina gave you?" I asked, feeling a little panicky about the trouble I was probably in myself.

Rose nodded dejectedly. "But it was my own

stupid fault for letting Amelia talk me into having the tattoo."

"I wonder what Bettina said about Tamsyn's tattoo?" I asked.

"*And* Amelia's," said Poppy.

"I bet Tamsyn was careful to keep hers hidden," said Rose. "And I suppose Bettina wouldn't mind about Amelia's because of permanent ones not marking things. All I know is that no way am I going to let Amelia get *you* into trouble, Jazz."

"Neither am I," said Poppy.

Although I gave them both a grateful smile, inside I was still worried what might happen to me, but not as worried as I felt about poor Miss Coralie.

7 Rose

Amelia made my blood boil. The more I thought about it, the more I felt sure that she'd deliberately gotten me into trouble with the tattoo. And now she was trying to get Jazz into trouble over her costume. I looked at her sitting with Tamsyn across the lunchroom. It was no wonder they'd made friends with each other. They were two nasty show-offs together.

I told myself to forget about the pair of them and concentrate on more important things, like those doll steps. I just hadn't been able to give up on them. I'd tried them out at home lots and lots, and the better I got, the more I wanted to show Don. Yes, I knew it was stupid when I was in trouble with Bettina, but even *that* didn't put me off my plan. Only I needed Poppy's and Jazz's help with what was on my mind, and I definitely didn't want any big ears tuning in to what I had to say, so I leaned forward and spoke in a low voice.

"What do you think Miss Coralie would have done if *she* were the choreographer of the *Nutcracker*, and she'd worked out a really good step, but no one could do it right?"

Poppy and Jazz frowned as they thought about that, but I couldn't wait a second longer for their answers. "I'll tell you what she'd do, she'd keep everyone working and working on her idea until she found someone who *could* do it."

Poppy must have seen where I was heading. She spoke in a tight, anxious voice. "You're not thinking of asking Don if you can try the doll steps *now*, are you?"

"You bet I am!" I answered, feeling excited and strong.

"I'm not sure it's such a good idea," Poppy then said a little shakily. "What do you think, Jasmine?"

Jazz spoke slowly. "Maybe if you were really, really careful about what you said to Don, Rose…and you chose the best possible moment to say it…"

Good, it looked as though Jazz understood how I felt. But Poppy was still wearing a deep frown.

"Are you thinking that Don will be mad?" I asked her.

"Yes. *And* Mr. Rivas. *And* Miss Farraday. *And* Miss Porter."

I could feel myself slumping down in my seat. I knew Poppy was right. And part of me also knew that it would be stupid and reckless to risk annoying Don, when I was already in trouble. But just when I was feeling as though I could slide right down to the floor with disappointment, Poppy suddenly sat up very straight and spoke in a firm voice. "All the same, I think you should do it, Rose. I think...Miss Coralie would want you to..." I nodded hard and felt a strange, nervous excitement welling up inside me.

"So, you'll do it then, Rose?" asked Jazz.

"For Miss Coralie?" said Poppy.

I didn't even hesitate. I was so much surer now that this was the right thing to do.

"Yes," I said firmly.

Jazz's eyes were shining as she put out her two thumbs. "Let's make a pact that every time we're dancing, no matter how old we are, and how long it is since we've seen Miss Coralie, we'll always do what we think she would want us to do."

"Yes. We'll keep her standards," said Poppy, pressing her own thumb against Jazz's.

Then I completed the circle. "For Miss Coralie, and for *us*."

✳

The twenty-second of December! Only two days till the first performance! And only three till Christmas Day!

Poppy, Jazz and I were sitting together in the back of Jazz's dad's car on our way to London, doing thumb-thumbs. We were talking in excited, nervous whispers about my plan to show Don the mechanical-doll steps. Today was my last chance.

"Remember, we're in it together," said Jazz. "If you get told off, Rose, Poppy and I will share the blame too."

Poppy nodded and her face looked pale under her freckles.

After that we were quiet for a while. I don't know about Poppy and Jazz, but I was wondering whether Sue was going to be angry at me for marking my costume with the tattoo, and worse still, whether Mr. Rivas had been told about it. Thinking these thoughts sent big shudders of fear through me, but I squeezed my eyes tight shut and tried to get rid of them so I could focus on my plan, which was the most important thing of all.

"I can't wait to rehearse onstage at the theater today," said Poppy. "It'll be so cool with the orchestra and lights and everything!"

"Sue said we'd be completely worn out by the end of the day, because of having to keep stopping and starting so we can get our placings right," said Jazz.

Poppy hugged herself and her eyes sparkled. "Well, I hope I'm not completely worn out because I've got presents to wrap when I get home."

"Me too," said Jazz.

So then we talked about what we wanted for Christmas and the cards and decorations we'd made, right up until we were traveling through the buzzing West End of London, when Christmassy stuff at home suddenly seemed nothing compared to the Christmas *Nutcracker*.

"Look!" I cried, spotting the big, colorful *NUTCRACKER* sign and *Ballet Theater UK* all in lights.

"The Princess Theater!" breathed Poppy, sitting bolt upright. "I can't believe that people who've actually paid to come and see us will be coming in through those very doors!"

"It's so golden and grand!" said Jazz, which I thought was a really good way of summing it up.

"Here's the stage door," said Jazz's dad, pulling up around the side of the theater. "Off you go, girls. Good luck."

And next minute, we were making our way in, talking excitedly about the number of famous people who must have gone in and out of the theater through this door over the years. The doorman called through to Sue and, while we waited for her to appear, we stared at all the photos of famous actors and dancers on the walls. Sue hurried us up some stairs and along a hallway to the dressing room. She seemed in a perfectly good mood and I decided that she couldn't have heard from Bettina yet about the mark on my costume.

I wasn't particularly looking forward to seeing Amelia today, but I knew I had to be sensible and grown-up, and just act normally, otherwise it would be even harder making myself smile at her in the Christmas Party scene. I looked around for her as soon as we went into the dressing room, but she hadn't arrived.

"It's not as nice as the changing room at the studios, is it?" said Tamsyn, wrinkling her nose at the threadbare carpet and the big old-fashioned heater.

I disagreed instantly. "It *is*!"

To me it felt magical. In fact it even *smelled* magical – of greasepaint and theater and fame. When we'd all changed into our ballet gear, Sue said it was time to go through to the wings. She ran her eye over us all. "Has anybody seen Sasha?"

Nobody had.

"What about Amelia?"

"I think she went to the bathroom," said Tamsyn.

"Hmm, she's been in there a while. Run and fetch her, dear," said Sue.

But Amelia walked in at that very moment, wearing her leotard and carrying her outdoor clothes in a bag.

"Oh! So you got changed in the bathroom, did you!" said Sue.

"It's not as if it's the dress rehearsal or anything. I didn't think it mattered," said Amelia.

"The rule is that you get changed in here where I can keep an eye on you all," said Sue. Then she looked around again and spoke briskly. "Right, let's get on our way."

"What about Sasha?" asked Laura.

"We'll have to start without her, I'm afraid."

"Sue treats us like babies, doesn't she?"

whispered Amelia to Tamsyn as we walked along the hallway.

"Sickening, isn't it?" said Tamsyn.

We three were just in front, but we ignored what Amelia and Tamsyn were saying.

"Just think, we're going to be dancing on a West End stage in a few minutes," whispered Poppy.

"I can't wait to stand in the wings," said Jazz. "Whenever I've dreamed of being a ballerina, I've always dreamed about the very moment when I step onto the stage from the wings."

"The wings are nothing special," Amelia chipped in. "You'll see."

Jazz and Poppy and I exchanged here-we-go-again looks. Amelia was still reminding us that she'd done it all before. But she was wrong about the wings. They *were* special. I just stared around me, especially at the stage, where most of the company dancers were silently stretching or practicing steps. They looked so perfectly in place, and I went off into a little dream about me being one of them and all the students wanting my autograph. Then I crept onto the stage and looked out into the magical theaterland. There were rows and rows of velvety seats, all deep red and bright gold with swirls and patterns that took my breath way. And the red swept up and up to the dark, gleaming wood of the front of the dress circle, and around to the plush gold boxes, and higher, to the upper circle and the silver and gold painted ceiling with its enormous chandeliers hanging like gigantic crystal balls, glinting and glittering down.

Then – *wham!* – I was back to earth with a jolt because Sue's cell phone was ringing. She answered it quickly and I could see her looking alarmed. When she disconnected, she went over to speak to Miss Farraday, who frowned and sucked in her lips. A moment later, both Miss Farraday and Sue returned to the wings.

"Bad news, girls. I'm afraid Sasha's not very

well," began Miss Farraday. "She's taking the day off to try and ensure that she'll definitely be well enough for the first performance. Laura, can you dance in the first cast for now? If you're feeling tired, we can get one of the others to stand in for you in the second cast."

Laura nodded, wide-eyed. "It's okay, I won't be tired. I can do it both times."

I knew I shouldn't be feeling happy about Sasha being ill, but I couldn't help the excitement that zipped its way up from my toes to my head. This could be my chance to ask Don if I could show him how I'd worked on the mechanical-doll solo.

Poppy was looking at Andy the pianist. "I thought the orchestra was going to be here," she whispered, sounding disappointed.

Sue must have heard her. "They'll be here this afternoon. You need the morning to get used to the stage, dear."

Then Mr. Rivas was explaining to us how he

wanted to make sure everyone knew their placings for the whole ballet in the morning, because in the afternoon it would be the technical rehearsal with the orchestra and the lighting. All the time he was talking, I was worrying that he might suddenly stop and say, "Oh yes, Rose Bedford, I want a word with you..." But he didn't, so then I started getting nervous at the thought of asking Don to watch my mechanical-doll imitation. It was going to be such a busy day with the adults concentrating on so many things. And I knew I had to be really careful, but I was determined to ask Don, because now I'd practiced hard at home, I knew I *could* do the steps. Anyway, it was my perfect chance; after all, no one could accuse me of trying to steal the limelight from Sasha. So I looked around for Don, but my heart started racing because he was nowhere in sight.

"Where's Don?" I asked Jazz in a panic. "I can't see him."

"First cast...in starting positions, please," said Mr. Rivas.

My eyes flew over the auditorium and then to the wings on either side. Don wasn't anywhere. I had to show him, though. It was all planned. For Miss Coralie.

My muscles were tightening up. It looked as though I'd left it too late. Unless...unless...I spoke to Mr. Rivas instead... After all, he was always making notes as we danced and talking to us afterward about how we could make the ballet even better by altering our placing very slightly or acting a little differently, and things like that.

I knew in my heart that this was different though. The points that Mr. Rivas wrote in his notebook were tiny details, not big sweeping changes to the choreography. And anyway, it was a big risk asking Mr. Rivas in case he suddenly realized that I was the girl who'd stupidly tattooed herself and messed up her costume.

"Forget about it for the moment," whispered Jazz urgently as we got into our places. "Just concentrate on dancing your best. We'll work something out afterward."

So that's what I did. I danced out of my skin, and smiled my biggest smile at Amelia when we were supposed to be having fun together. There was a lot of stopping and starting to get us in exactly the right place at the right time, but at the end of the party scene, Mr. Rivas clapped from the auditorium and said he was pleasantly surprised and had thought there would be many more hitches than that. He praised the company dancers, then told us students that our dancing had been excellent.

"I just want you to remember that every step you dance, every gesture you make, every expression on your face, *really* counts," he said. "That was fine for a first rehearsal onstage, but for a performance you need to pull the very last shred of energy from deep inside you and give it to the audience..." He beamed around at the second cast sitting in the auditorium, then turned back to us. "...even when there is only a tiny audience."

Everyone laughed and I realized that Mr. Rivas was in a great mood. This might be my only opportunity. I had to screw up all my courage and make myself say something. Right now. I had one last look around for Don, but there was still no sign of him. I noticed Jazz's eyes though. They were big and round and thoughtful, but not giving me any clue about what she was actually thinking, even when I raised my eyebrows at her.

"All right, Rose?" asked Mr. Rivas suddenly. He must have seen me looking around.

Should I just nod and say I'm fine?

Should I go for it and say what I'd planned to say to Don?

Would it ruin everything?

Should I wait till Don arrives?

126

Will I ever get this opportunity again?
What would Miss Coralie say?

And that's when I knew that I had to do it. "Ahh...I'm really sorry to disturb you when you're so busy, but I've been practicing the original choreography where one of the children imitates the mechanical doll..."

I heard Amelia gasp and Tamsyn whisper, "Huh! Show-off!"

But I made myself ignore them and keep on. "And I know it's late to be asking you, but I wondered if you'd like to see if you think it might...give more energy to the audience..."

My shoulders were so tense that I didn't think I'd ever be able to relax them again. Mr. Rivas had narrowed his eyes until they were almost shut. It was impossible to tell if he was looking at me or at the stage in general. The whole auditorium was silent, waiting to hear what he said.

Then he suddenly dropped his notepad to his

side. "All right. Let's take a look... Give Rose four bars please, Andy..."

Yesss! Now I had to make the most of this chance.

The rest of the students and the dancers moved back quickly to give me enough space, and I shot to the place where I thought I should be and quickly shook out my body to get rid of my tenseness. This was going to be so amazing. In the few seconds before the piano started I got the clearest picture in my head of Mr. Rivas leaping onto the stage with a massive smile on his face and his arms flung wide as he told me he'd get the choreography changed back immediately. I was so fired up that the moment the music started I felt as though I could do anything. I don't know if this was a different type of piano from the one in the studio, but it sounded more powerful, and Andy was making the music really staccato and sharp, which gave me even more energy. Then, when I came to the slow *développé*, he drew out the music so it seemed to shiver as I turned into the *arabesque*, and finally I slapped my hands on the floor and dropped into the splits.

I'd done it. I was still staring right ahead with my palms turned up and everyone was clapping, but I couldn't decide whether it would be more professional to stay in position until the clapping had stopped or whether that would be seen as showing off. In the end I just waited for a few seconds, then jumped up and stood there feeling stupid while I waited for Mr. Rivas to say something. Poppy's eyes were sparkling as she gave me a small nod to tell me I'd done all right.

But then all my happiness and energy started to seep away because Mr. Rivas hardly moved. "Thank you, Rose," he said, looking up at me carefully when the clapping stopped. "You certainly have been practicing..." He took a deep breath and I suddenly felt like a silly little girl because I knew what was coming.

"We'll crack on with the rehearsal I think, but yes…thank you for showing me."

So that was it. I'd done it. It was all over. I hadn't been told off or anything, but I obviously hadn't danced well enough because I hadn't managed to convince Mr. Rivas that it would be better to change the choreography back. I sighed and felt so disappointed I could hardly be bothered to make my way to a seat in the front row. And what about the clapping? Was everyone just being kind? That thought made me furious. I didn't want people to feel sorry for me. I wanted to be good enough. I should have practiced more. Yes, that's what was wrong. I could have kicked myself for not practicing more.

Jazz whispered that I'd done brilliantly, but at the same time I heard Amelia mumble the word "show-off", and I knew she was talking about me. As the second cast got into their positions, I sat there in a tight, sad little ball, hugging my knees up to my chest. Then Sue went rushing up to Mr. Rivas, looking very anxious, and spoke to him in low whispers for a few seconds.

"Miss Farraday, Miss Porter... Could I have a word, please?" said Mr. Rivas as soon as Sue had finished.

They hurried to his side. By now, everyone was wondering what on earth had happened.

We didn't have to wait long to find out. "Listen up, students," said Mr. Rivas in a serious voice. "I'm afraid Sasha's mother has called again. It seems that Sasha's not just under the weather. She's really sick. The doctor thinks it's a virus of some sort, so clearly she's not going to be well enough to dance until after Christmas. Now, we've decided it's just too short notice to bring in a reserve student and expect them to learn such a lot of steps, so we're going to swap one of the second cast students into the first cast, then Sasha can fill that person's place in the second cast in the new year. We'll make our decision about who to swap when we've had time to talk to Don and to consider it very carefully."

Tamsyn's hand shot up and she spoke in a gabble. "Excuse me, Mr. Rivas, I could easily learn Sasha's part in *Waltz of the Flowers* and I'd love to be in the first cast."

"Yes, Tamsyn would fit in really well," said Amelia.

"As I say, we'll make the decision in due course," Mr. Rivas replied evenly.

I glanced at Poppy on the stage. Her face was pink and her eyes were glittering. I couldn't tell if she was anxious or excited.

"It would be so cool if Poppy was chosen to swap into the first cast," Jazz whispered to me.

But I knew we mustn't get our hopes up because it was obvious that Tamsyn was desperate to be with Amelia, and knowing those two, they'd find a way to make that happen.

"It'd be better than cool. It'd be the best thing in the world," I whispered back. Then we did a thumb-thumb, each of us making our silent wishes.

8 Poppy

When Mr. Rivas first told us that someone would be swapping from the second cast into the first, I felt an enormous shock that sent a wave of excitement whizzing through every part of me. But now I just feel flat because I'm so sure they're going to choose Tamsyn. You see, Mr. Rivas has just asked her to try Sasha's part in the *Waltz of the Flowers* and, I have to admit, she did it really well.

The orchestra arrived at lunchtime for the technical rehearsal this afternoon. I love being so close to the players and I never realized how important the conductor is. I imagine him as a puppeteer, and the musicians as the puppets, playing his tune.

When it was the second cast's turn to dance *Waltz of the Flowers,* I hurried to my position and closed my eyes to get myself ready. Now that it was the orchestra playing, and not Andy on the piano, the music seemed to shimmer all over the stage like a fine mist, and I felt as though I was dancing on the mist. I really seemed to come alive at last. This was the best feeling I'd had since we'd started rehearsing on the very first day, and it stayed with me even after the music stopped and we were holding our final shapes.

"Lovely!" said Mr. Rivas, looking at Miss Porter to see if she was happy.

"Stunning!" she said, breaking into a smile, which is rare for Miss Porter.

"Absolutely," added Miss Farraday.

"All right, I think you students deserve a

break, then we'll meet up again in about forty-five minutes, Sue," Mr. Rivas said.

All three of the artistic staff were beaming like crazy as Sue nodded and beckoned to us from the wings. But Mr. Rivas called me back and I crouched down at the front of the stage. He was standing in the auditorium.

"I knew you could do it, Poppy." He smiled. "You just needed an orchestra, didn't you!"

I nodded hard and felt so relieved that after all my worrying, it was something as simple as that. For this one particular piece of music that I love the most in the world, the piano really couldn't bring me to life.

"Well done, Poppy! That was lovely," said a voice beside him, and I realized I was being praised by Lisette Canning.

"Thank you v-very much," I managed to stammer.

Then I hurried to catch up with Jazz and Rose, who were waiting for me in the wings.

Tamsyn was there too, wearing a big scowl.

"Did he ask you to swap into the first cast?" she snapped.

"No, he just said that I'd done well."

Immediately, the scowl dropped off her face and she plunged after Amelia. I could see them whispering together, then giving each other the thumbs-up sign, so I guess Tamsyn was telling Amelia that it was okay, I hadn't been asked to swap.

I'd been full of a wonderful golden feeling a moment before, but now it was just as though someone had come along and rubbed the shine off my happiness. If only I could dance in the first cast then everything would be perfect.

9 Jasmine

Poppy and Rose had gone on ahead to the changing room, but I'd stopped for a moment to do up one of the drawstrings on my ballet shoes, which had come loose. And then I heard someone saying my name.

"It's Jasmine, isn't it?"

I turned and immediately felt my face flooding with color. It was the dancer I'd seen in the bathroom when I'd been imitating a mechanical doll in front of the mirror, the one who was in the lunchroom when Amelia had banged into the tray I was carrying. She probably thought I was responsible for messing up Amelia's costume. I so wished I'd just left my drawstring and gone back to the changing room with the others.

"I'm Kirsty...Kirsty Reeve," she said.

Surprisingly, she sounded really friendly. All the same, my heart was beating faster because I still didn't want to talk to her. It just seemed so unfair that twice she'd seen me looking stupid. It was embarrassing enough when she'd come into the bathroom, but what had happened in the lunchroom was much worse than that. I hated to think that people might be blaming me for messing up Amelia's costume, when it absolutely wasn't my fault. I was just about to start explaining things, when she put her hand on my shoulder and gave me a big smile.

"I'm glad I've caught you on your own. I've been wanting to talk to you. You see, I know you've seen me looking at you once or twice and

I didn't want you to think I was being rude...
It's just that you remind me of someone. That
first time I ever saw you...you know, when you
were in the bathroom?"

"I was only trying to see if I could look like a
mechanical doll."

"Yes, I know, but what was so weird was that
when I was your age I was dancing in
Nutcracker with the Royal Ballet, and almost
exactly the same thing happened to me!"

I looked at her more closely then. "I remind
you of *yourself*!"

"Yes! I was in the bathroom on my own and I
started dancing the role of Clara. I was smiling
at myself in the mirror, pretending to receive the
gift of the nutcracker from Drosselmeyer, and
that was when one of the Royal Ballet dancers
came in and saw me. It was such a coincidence
seeing you lost in your own little world, doing
that smiling thing, that I just had to tell my
friends. The difference was that the dancer who

saw me really *was* playing the role of Clara. She was the best soloist in the company. You can imagine, I felt so embarrassed."

"I know the feeling!"

Kirsty started laughing at that point, so we had to move even farther back in the wing in case we disturbed the dancing onstage. When she'd recovered, she said, "Anyway, I think you've got really good technique."

A wave of happiness came over me. "Really? Do you?" But then my panic about what had happened in the lunchroom came rushing to the surface and, before I could stop myself, I was blurting out my side of the story, because I wondered if Kirsty might be able to help me by telling Mr. Rivas that it really hadn't been my fault.

"It's okay, you don't have to explain," she interrupted when I'd hardly started. "I saw it all and reported it to Bettina. I tell you, she was in a red-hot fury with Amelia because there was so much really careful cleaning to do on her dress."

It felt as though a huge weight had been lifted off me, leaving me as light as a feather. And I couldn't believe what a good actress Amelia had been. No one would ever have guessed that she'd just gotten in so much trouble when she'd come back to the lunchroom. But I didn't care about that. It was just such a relief to know that *I* wasn't in trouble.

"I'll be able to dance without worrying now," I told Kirsty happily.

"It's such a shame that you've had that on your mind all this time," said Kirsty, looking at me kindly. "That girl Amelia was a pain last year, but she seems even worse this year. The trouble is, she manages to kid the staff that she's a goodie two shoes!"

"She *is* a good dancer though," I said.

"Not as good as you," said Kirsty. "I think you've got the makings of a soloist. Where do you train?"

"The Coralie Charlton School of Ballet," I told her proudly.

She gasped when I said that. "That's incredible! Coralie Charlton is the dancer who caught me pretending to be Clara!" Kirsty and I stared at each other, wide-eyed with surprise. "So, how is she? I've thought about her often over the years, and wondered what she's doing. But now I know!" She grinned. "Turning out fine dancers like you."

Such a feeling of sadness came over me at that moment that I thought I was going to burst into tears. I spoke in a very shaky voice.

"She's not very well, actually... In fact, she's in the hospital with pneumonia."

"Oh no!" Kirsty's hands flew to her mouth.

In my mind I went over the conversation I'd had with Maman the previous evening. Maman had promised me that Miss Coralie was getting better and she might even be out of the hospital in time for Christmas, but I still didn't know whether she was just saying that to stop me worrying about her. It was such a shame that Miss Coralie wouldn't be able to watch our first performance.

"My mom thinks she'll only be in the hospital for a few more days," I said.

"Let's hope she's well enough to enjoy Christmas," said Kirsty. "Do give her my love when you see her. She won't know who on earth Kirsty Reeve is, but if you just say it's the girl who pretended she was Clara, she'll remember!"

"Yes, I'll tell her. Of course I will," I said.

Then Kirsty reached for my hand and gave it a squeeze. "I'd better go now. I'll see you later."

My heart squeezed too at that moment...with happiness. *And* with sadness.

10 Rose

The door to the changing room opened and in came Jazz, looking really flushed and excited about something.

"Where did you get to?" I asked her, but she didn't get the chance to reply because Sue clapped her hands and spoke in a deadly serious voice.

"Stop what you're doing, please. Listen carefully. This is very important and I need everyone's attention. Yesterday, Bettina came to see me." I felt the blood draining from my face. "She showed me a red mark on a costume and

I was appalled to hear that Rose had stupidly put a tattoo on her back." My heart was banging, but I made myself keep looking right at Sue, even though I knew everyone was staring at me, while inside my head a little prayer was going on. *Please don't say I've been thrown out...*

Sue's eyes were angrier than I'd ever seen them as she asked me to show her my back. I'd washed the tattoo off the night before, so I quickly rolled down my leotard, put a top on and rushed over at top speed mumbling that I was sorry, and waiting to hear what she said next. But she just looked at my back, gave me a quick nod and started talking to everyone again, so I scuttled back to Jazz and Poppy.

"I can't believe that after all I said about how precious the costumes are, something like this has happened. If there is anyone else in this room who has a tattoo anywhere on their body, you must tell me right now." Her eyes scanned slowly around everyone and I took a quick glance at Tamsyn and Amelia to see if they were going to own up. Amelia was edging back toward the bench where her bag was, but Tamsyn caught me looking at her, and pulled her face into a big sneer. "I washed mine off before my costume fitting because *I'm* sensible." Then I distinctly heard a snicker coming from Amelia's direction and when my eyes met hers I saw a big look of triumph there that made me sick. It was obvious that she and Tamsyn had set me up to get in trouble from the beginning. And they'd succeeded too, because I'd been in terrible trouble and I still didn't know if there was worse to come.

I was just plucking up the courage to ask Sue whether Mr. Rivas had been told about my tattoo, when Jazz suddenly blurted something out that made everyone gasp. "I don't know why you're looking at Rose like that, Amelia, because she's not the only one to get told off, is she?"

Amelia's eyes darted around as though she was searching for what to say, then she turned back to Jazz. "It's nothing to do with you, Jasmine Ayed."

Sue spoke angrily. "Oh, but it is, Amelia! You were trying to put the blame for your stupid behavior on poor Jasmine, weren't you? But, thank goodness, one of the dancers told Bettina the truth about what happened in the lunchroom."

Amelia's eyes widened in shock.

"You may well look ashamed, young lady," Sue went on. "Bettina told me the whole story. The only reason I haven't said anything to you is because you've been so thoroughly told off by both Bettina and Mr. Rivas."

Amelia turned red then, and I thought for a moment that she was going to burst into tears because everyone was staring at her. But she just tossed her head and started drinking her juice.

I think Tamsyn must have been feeling sorry

for her because she tried to get the attention off her by sighing and asking Sue, "Do we have to stay here for our break? There's nothing to do."

Sue's eyes flashed and she sounded as though she was only just managing to keep her temper. "I haven't finished yet. And the reason we're here, Tamsyn, is because some people wanted a snack and we're not allowed to eat or drink in the auditorium." We all stayed completely still as she wrote something in her notebook. "I am reporting back to Bettina that she definitely won't find any more tattoos." Then she looked up and scanned around the room one last time as if to make totally sure that this was true.

I looked at Amelia again, but she was fiddling in her bag.

Tamsyn must have seen me looking. "Amelia's is *permanent*," she said with a sneer. "*Permanent* tattoos don't come off, okay?"

Sue looked up sharply from her notebook.

"I didn't know anything about a permanent tattoo. Has Bettina seen it?"

"What?" said Amelia vaguely. "Oh, yeah. She said it was fine."

Sue's eyes narrowed. "You'd better show me. After what's happened, I'm not taking any risks."

"Can I show you after, Sue?" asked Amelia in her politest voice.

Sue hesitated. "Just put on a top like Rose did. I want an end to this matter right now."

Amelia rolled her eyes at Tamsyn, then looked calmly at Sue. "I had it removed."

"I see," said Sue. "I shall have to make sure all the same." So Amelia had to show Sue, and this time her face was bright red. I wasn't surprised. Lots of people were whispering and one or two were even snickering. It was so obvious that no one believed Amelia had ever had a tattoo in the first place.

I waited a few minutes till everyone was chatting normally again and eating their snacks, and Sue was sitting on her own reading something, then I crept over to her.

"Excuse me, Sue," I said quietly, "but can you tell me whether I've been reported to Mr. Rivas?"

Sue must have been feeling in a better mood by then because she actually gave me a half smile. "Don't worry, Rose. I think you've learned your lesson, haven't you?"

I nodded.

"Well, then. Nothing more will be said on the subject. You just concentrate on doing your best dancing now."

I felt like hugging her I was so happy. "Yes, I will." I nodded harder. "I really will."

It was the end of the day and we were all getting changed to go home, but I was still in my leotard, sitting there, wrapped up in angry thoughts about Amelia, my brain going at a hundred and fifty miles an hour. If it hadn't been for her shaking her head at me, I would have asked Don in the first place if I could try out for the doll solo. I was certain he would have thought I'd be able to manage it as long as I practiced. But I'd stupidly believed Amelia was doing me a favor warning me not to volunteer, and now I finally knew how hateful that girl was, I was kicking myself for ever thinking anything different. She'd made me blow my chances of doing something that Miss Coralie would have wanted me to do, and I could never forgive her for that.

Then suddenly, like a shining beacon, the most amazing thought shone out. Immediately I grabbed Poppy and Jazz and spoke to them in a whisper.

"I'm going to have another try at the mechanical-doll steps."

Poppy looked alarmed. "What, now? Where?"

"On the stage. I'm furious with myself for not being able to convince Mr. Rivas before. I obviously didn't do it perfectly. Anyway, Mr. Rivas said that Don would be here tomorrow and I want one last try to convince him, so I need to practice first."

"But it's the dress rehearsal tomorrow," said Poppy, in a squeak. "That's too late!"

"And you can't go on the stage!" whispered Jazz, her eyes wide.

"No, you can't," Poppy agreed. "Not without permission."

But now I'd gotten the idea in my head and I couldn't let it go. "It'll be okay, don't worry," I whispered. "Only, I need you two to keep guard in the wings."

"What?" cried Poppy.

"No, we can't!" hissed Jazz.

They looked terrified, and I knew I'd never be able to get them to agree, but this was my last chance, so I'd just have to do it anyway and pray that no one came along and caught me. So I got up to go, but my heart missed a beat because Tamsyn was staring at me. Surely she hadn't heard what I'd been saying? No, she couldn't have done. I'd been speaking too softly, hadn't I...?

A few moments later, I was tiptoeing along the hallway toward the wings. There was no sign of anyone. I thought I heard a noise though, so I crept onto the stage to make sure that the orchestra had definitely all gone. They had. Then I heard another noise from behind me. My eyes shot back to the wing.

"We couldn't leave you on your own," said Poppy.

"But you'll have to be really quick," added Jazz, "because we'll be in so much trouble if we get caught."

"Thanks," I said, feeling an enormous burst of gratitude toward my best friends. "Cough if anyone shows up."

They were standing like tense soldiers in the wing as I went to my starting position, singing the music inside my head to get myself prepared. It felt so amazing to have the whole stage to myself. I bounced and twirled and threw myself around, jumping higher than ever on the scissor jumps. There was no need to remind myself to keep it jerky because everything felt completely natural now, and I knew I was perfectly balanced for the *développé*. Turning into the *arabesque* is the hardest part of all, because you have to try and keep your leg at the same height as for the *développé*, but I concentrated with all my might and felt sure that I'd managed it. Then I did the same with the other leg, and finally dropped into the splits.

"That was so…"

But I never did find out what Jazz was going to say because Poppy suddenly gasped and looked around.

"We *knew* you were up to something," came Tamsyn's loud voice. And a second later, she and Amelia had pushed past Jazz and Poppy and were marching onto the stage as though they owned it.

"You're breaking the rules!" said Amelia, her hands on her waist and her eyes flashing furiously.

I was just about to say, so are *you,* when we all froze at the sound of Don's voice in the other wing. "Let me be the judge of that."

He walked onto the stage very slowly, head down, staring at the ground.

"We only came to tell Rose and the others they weren't allowed on the stage with no adults present," said Tamsyn, who had instantly changed to her politest voice.

"Thank you," said Don. He looked at Amelia and back to Tamsyn. "You can both go then..." He said the next words very deliberately. "...since an adult is now present."

Amelia and Tamsyn looked startled, and stared at Don for a while as if to make sure that he definitely did mean them to go. "Wh-what about Poppy and Jasmine? Sh-should they go too?" said Tamsyn.

But Don seemed to be deep in thought and Tamsyn had to say it again. This time Don answered rather sharply.

"No, I need a word with Poppy."

He hadn't mentioned Jasmine, but Tamsyn and Amelia obviously decided it would be better not to risk saying anything else, because they scuttled off like two little mice. Jazz moved closer to Poppy then as though she wanted to protect her, and I noticed Poppy's face looked like wax. I think my face was probably as pale as that too because I was so worried about what was going to happen to me. I'd been idiotic coming onto the stage when it's strictly out of bounds, and I guessed Don was only staring at the floor so he could try and find some words that would be strong enough to tell me how mad at me he was. And right in the middle of that scary thought I got a shock, because Mr. Rivas suddenly appeared from the wing opposite.

"There you are, Don!" he said, striding onstage. "I was wanting a word..." But he stopped when he saw me. "Aha, you've found Rose already." He threw me a quick smile, then continued talking to Don. "I was coming to tell you that this young lady gave me a pretty convincing performance this afternoon of those steps you wanted in the first act."

My heart began to beat faster.

"I've just seen it," said Don. Then he turned to me. "I'm only here by chance, actually. I don't usually come to final rehearsals because the choreography has long since been sorted out, but it looks like I should have been here today after all. The staff are full of your performance, Rose, and now I've seen it for myself I can tell why! Anyway, it's the dress rehearsal tomorrow, which means that we've still got time to put that solo in..."

I couldn't believe what I was hearing.

"You mean you're actually going to let me do the doll steps?"

"Absolutely. You're a natural!"

"Oh, wicked!" I said, and my voice rang around the auditorium.

The two men burst out laughing, but I just smiled and smiled while my heart sang.

11 Poppy

I'd been terrified that Rose was going to be in big trouble for going on the stage and I thought Jasmine and I might get in trouble too, so it was just wonderful when Don told Rose that he was going to let her do the doll solo. But there was another surprise to come. Right out of the blue, Mr. Rivas suddenly turned to me and said, "Poppy, we'd like you to swap into the first cast if that's all right with you…"

I was so stunned, I couldn't speak. There must have been some mistake. My mind shot back to the time, even before the first rehearsal had begun, when Miss Farraday had told us which casts we were in, and Tamsyn had asked if we were allowed to swap. I can still remember Mr. Rivas's answer as if it had been only ten minutes ago. *"The casts have been selected carefully. It's all about coloring, height, the way you dance..."*

And now Mr. Rivas was saying that he wanted me to swap into the first cast, but I absolutely mustn't get excited because he couldn't have thought it through fully and any minute now he might suddenly realize he'd made a mistake. The thought of being able to dance in the same performances as Jasmine and Rose was like the most wonderful gift, and it would be unbearable if I suddenly had it taken away from me, so I stayed completely still and quiet.

Rose wasn't quiet though. "Yes, it *is* all right!" she squealed. "Incredibly magnificently *perfectly* all right." She turned to me, eyes wide, nodding hard. *"Isn't* it, Poppy?"

I just managed to nod.

"Are you sure, Poppy?" asked Mr. Rivas gently. "We don't have to change you over if you're not happy about it…"

So then I had to speak. But how could I explain? "I…really want to swap, but…are you sure I'm not too…tall?"

Don and Mr. Rivas exchanged puzzled looks, and I looked down as Rose sighed dramatically.

It was Jazz who came to the rescue. "One of the students has been saying to Poppy that she was only given her role in the first act because she's the same height as Lisette Canning. And it's made Poppy worry that she's no good at dancing…"

"Even though we've told her she's great," Rose finished off.

"Poppy," said Mr. Rivas firmly, so I had to look up. "Your friends are right. You can be very proud indeed of the way you dance. And all the artistic staff have seen what a strong bond there is between you three girls, so we know we're making the right decision in having you dancing together in the same cast."

I felt as though I'd been shivering in the darkness and suddenly a warm bright sun had magically appeared. At last I managed to smile, and Mr. Rivas looked relieved. "That's better," he said.

"All *three* of you have got a great deal of potential," added Don. "We can tell who your teacher is!"

Rose, Jazz and I looked at each other in amazement. It was unbelievable. Even the adults knew where we went to ballet school.

Mr. Rivas sounded brisk and excited now. "Right you'd better get along. Big day tomorrow! Dress rehearsal."

But I was transfixed. I couldn't move. I was staring out at the enormous auditorium. This wasn't the first time I'd seen it, of course, but it was the first time I'd really looked at it closely. In two days' time, every seat would be filled.

And *I* would be dancing with Rose and Jasmine. It was going to be wonderful. But then a wave of sadness came over me because I'd been picturing Miss Coralie looking up with her bright eyes watching us, only she wouldn't be there. I tried to tell myself that it didn't make any difference because you can't see anything except darkness when the lights are shining on the stage. But I was kidding myself. I did *so* wish she could be there, so I made a resolution that I'd just have to imagine her. Then I concentrated on dreaming about the bright beams of the spotlights, shining and polishing our dancing.

Just two days.

I couldn't wait.

I really couldn't.

12 Jasmine

This is the most exciting moment of my life. Even when I was lucky enough to do a class once with the Rambert Dance Company, it wasn't as incredible as this. Today is Christmas Eve, and Poppy, Rose and I are, at this precise moment, walking into the Princess Theater through the stage door. We've just been around to the front of the theater and it's absolutely buzzing with people waiting to go in, even though there's over an hour until curtain-up.

"I'm scared!" said Poppy for the sixty-sixth time.

"You're squeaking again!" said Rose, and we all burst out laughing.

We went upstairs and walked along to the dressing room. It seemed half-empty now there was only one cast there instead of two.

"Hello, you three." Sue smiled. "Got your best dancing feet with you?"

We hardly answered her because our eyes had flown to the rack of costumes. They lit up the room with all their beautiful colors. We knew we weren't supposed to touch them more than we had to, which was a shame because I felt like running my fingers through the lace and silk and the soft, floaty tulle, so the bright sequins sparkled and shimmered in the light.

Sue started helping us to get changed. I've worn a few different costumes for Miss Coralie's shows, but none of them has given me the same incredible feeling that my *Nutcracker* costume gave me. My dress is silky and goes down to the middle of my calves. It's ivory-colored with a silver sash and tulle petticoats that make it flare out. Sue helped me with the hooks and eyes at the back, then the assistant wig mistress, who's called Mahin, arrived to help with headdresses and to do our make-up.

Rose snickered as she had her make-up put on. "Sorry," she said. "It just feels funny." When she saw herself in the mirror, her eyes flew open. "Haven't I got too much on? My face looks nearly orange!"

"Don't worry, you'll look perfect onstage," said Mahin. "The lights are so bright, you need plenty of color."

When it was Poppy's turn, she had even more make-up than Rose to cover all her freckles, but I didn't need much at all because I've already got fairly dark skin.

"You all look gorgeous!" said Sue. "Now, where are those cameras? Get in a group and I'll take your photos for you."

It was Sue who'd suggested that everyone

brought their cameras. "You'll want a memory of the magical time just before you go onstage, girls," she'd said the day before when we'd all been getting changed to go home at the end of the dress rehearsal.

When poor Sue had taken eleven photos with eleven different cameras and when we'd all smiled and said "cheese" eleven times we started gently limbering up and stretching our muscles, but after a few minutes there was a knock on the door. It was the stage doorman. "Just been delivered," he said, handing an envelope to Sue.

Sue smiled. "Poppy, Jasmine and Rose, looks like you've got a good-luck card from someone."

Poppy took it and everyone gathered around except Amelia.

"I've left all my cards at home," she said.

No one took any notice at all of that comment because all eyes were on Poppy opening the envelope. The three of us started to read the card together, our voices low and

puzzled at first, then stronger and higher as we
became more and more excited.

>   *To Poppy, Jasmine and Rose,*
>   *I wish you all the very best of luck.*
>   *I know you'll be wonderful.*
>   *I'll see you at the end.*
>   *With much love,*
>   *Miss Coralie xxx*

"Miss Coralie!" we all squealed.

"Oh, that's so cool," said Rose.

"I can't believe she's better," I said.

"Who *is* she?" asked Lizzie.

"Our ballet teacher, Coralie Charlton," said
Poppy in another one of her squeals.

"Oh, wow! I've heard of Coralie Charlton!
Lucky you, having her as your teacher!"

And we *were* lucky. More lucky than Lizzie
knew. More lucky than even Rose and Poppy
knew. I let my breath out slowly. I could finally

stop worrying because Miss Coralie was out of hospital and right *here* in this building. She was actually sitting somewhere in the auditorium waiting for the curtain to rise. The relief I felt was so strong that I wanted to cry with happiness, but then over the speaker came the voice of the stage manager: "Beginners, please." And from that moment on I only wanted to fly.

The stage manager had given us four warning calls over the speaker telling us there were thirty minutes to go, then ten, then five and this last one which meant that everyone who was on at the beginning of the ballet should make their way to the wings right away because the curtain was about to go up. "Right," said Sue. "Time to go!" And a shiver of nervous excitement raced around the room.

"You'll all be wonderful!" said Sue, beaming. "Come on, let's get this show on the road. Not a sound from now on."

She didn't have to tell us.

13 Rose

Even though we'd had the technical rehearsal and were used to the lights, nothing prepared me for the feeling I got when I first stepped onto the stage. The atmosphere was more magical than at any rehearsal because everything was complete – every last drop of make-up, every puff of hairspray, every brand new *pointe* shoe, every single note of music that rang around the theater and drew the audience into our Christmas Nutcracker world on the stage.

As I danced with the others at the beginning of the party scene, I could feel the energy building up inside me for my solo. I wondered if there would be any laughter from the auditorium. Mr. Rivas said that if I did it really well, the audience would immediately realize what I was doing and hopefully find it amusing. My feet tingled as I lined up to receive my Christmas present from the dancers playing the roles of Clara's parents. My smile was the biggest ever when it came to the part where Amelia and I pretend to be playing a trick.

Then it was time for my solo and my whole body felt alive as I began to imitate the jerky movements of the mechanical doll. Immediately, a burst of laughter came from the blackness of the auditorium, which spurred me on to throw myself into the steps like never before. I kept my legs very straight for the bounces and the scissor leaps, and really extended my back for the flop-over. Then I got my balance for the *développés* and finally dropped into the sideways splits with my head on one side and my palms up. And that was when I got a shock because loud clapping broke out. I couldn't believe my ears, but I didn't have even a second to think about it because the music continued and so did the dancing. The rest of the party scene seemed to flash by I was on such a high, and then we were flying into the wings because it was time for the mice to do their dance.

"Oh, wasn't it absolutely fantastic!" I whispered to Poppy as we walked back to the changing room.

Poppy squeaked a reply. "I wonder if the audience liked it?"

"Well, someone did," said Jazz. "Didn't you hear that big whistle from the circle?"

I was keeping quiet. I thought I knew precisely who was responsible for that whistle, and I wasn't sure if it was allowed at ballets.

Poppy looked at my face and guessed. "Was it Rory?"

I made a face and nodded. "My brothers let me down wherever I go!"

"You should feel pleased to have brothers who are so proud of you, Rose," Sue said.

"But whistling? At a ballet?"

"Yes, why not?" Sue laughed. "Now let's get you changed into your tutus for Act Two."

14 Poppy

My favorite part of the whole ballet was when we danced *Waltz of the Flowers*. The music rose up from the orchestra and instantly I felt that beautiful mist filling the air.

The lights wrapped us up in a cocoon on the stage and the company dancers seemed to be reaching out and folding us five girls into their midst. We were all floating together on the shimmering music, and when it ended, the feeling inside me was like soft, warm peace with a frosting of magic.

A second later, though, the peace was

shattered because thunderous clapping filled the auditorium and for once the conductor waited, his baton aloft, and the orchestra sat up straight, the violinists with their bows poised. Then the finale began. And from that point until the end of the ballet, there was so much clapping that at times it almost drowned out the music.

As the last chord was struck, a huge cheer filled the theater and the audience rose to its feet. Three people came onto the stage with bouquets of flowers. Two of them were for Lisette and one for Carly, the Sugarplum Fairy.

The clapping seemed to get louder still as Don came onstage and took a bow. Then everyone curtsyed or bowed again and again and again, just as we'd been taught, as the clapping went on and on.

When the curtain finally came down, I wished we could dance the whole ballet all over again. The five *Waltz of the Flowers* students all hugged each other and then the dancers were hugging us too. Lisette was already heading for her changing room, but she suddenly came back and gave me my own special hug.

"I can't forget my lovely dancing friend," she said.

In the changing room, everyone was talking loudly and excitedly. Sue was blobbing cold cream on our faces and handing out cotton balls. "Just get the face make-up off," she said, "and take great care with the costumes. We don't want a single mark on them."

Then the doorman rang Sue's cell phone to tell her that parents and friends were beginning to arrive at the stage door to see us, and that made us all rush around trying to get changed even faster. Some of the girls started to leave, shouting, "Happy Christmas, everyone! Don't eat too much Christmas candy!"

"Oh, help! I can't find my camera!" said Rose, jumping around with one shoe on.

Jasmine and I were ready, but we put down

our bags and joined in the search as more and more girls went to meet their parents till finally we were the only ones left.

"Look! It's under this bench. It must have got kicked there!" laughed Rose.

"Off you go then, girls," said Sue with a smile. "Happy Christmas."

"Happy Christmas, Sue!"

And we plunged into the hallway, but stopped immediately because there, coming toward us were all our parents, arms outstretched to give us hugs. Rose got high-fived by her big brothers, and my little brother, Stevie, decided to imitate them. For about a minute, everyone talked non-stop. But then I happened to look farther down the hallway and my heart started racing.

"Jasmine! Rose! Look!" I cried.

Everyone stopped talking and turned to follow my gaze. Miss Coralie and a man who must be her husband were walking along the hallway toward us.

Like magic, our families made a way through for her and that's when we saw her clearly. She looked tinier than ever, wearing a slim-fitting, jade green dress with boots and a little jacket like a beautiful model, her dark hair loose around her shoulders, her eyes glittering like coals in her pale face. And when she smiled at us, I felt like bursting into tears of joy.

"Thank you for the card," said Jasmine.

"We've been thinking about you," I said.

"And trying to imagine you were with us all the time," said Rose.

"We've got so much to tell you," I added.

Miss Coralie came forward to give us all hugs and I smelled her perfume and saw that she had tears in her eyes too. "I can't wait to hear everything!" she said. Then she took a step back. "You did me proud this evening," she said quietly. "I felt as though I had a little glimpse of future fame for my three flowers!"

None of us knew what to say after that. It

was the best compliment ever. Even the adults stayed quiet for a few seconds until Jasmine's dad broke the silence.

"They certainly were wonderful, weren't they? And I think they deserve a treat. Shall we all go and find a restaurant?"

Everyone thought that was a great idea.

"We'll drink a toast!" said my dad. "To our three girls!"

"And future fame!" said Rose's eldest brother, Adam.

I loved those words. And so did Jasmine and Rose.

Our moms and Miss Coralie went into the dressing room to thank Sue, while the rest of our families started to make their way back toward the stairs that led down to the stage door.

But we three just stood there and pressed our thumbs together.

"Future fame…" we whispered, looking at each other with sparkling eyes.

And our words seem to hang there in the magical air of the Princess Theater, leaving their own little message.

This could be it. The Christmas Nutcracker. The beginning of three ballerina dreams coming true.

❋   ❋   ✳   ✳   ❋   ❋

Basic Ballet Positions

First position

Second position

Third position

Fourth position

Fifth position

Ballet words are mostly in French, which makes them more magical. But when you're learning, it's good to know what they mean too. Here are some of the words that all Miss Coralie's students have to learn:

adage The name for the slow steps in the center of the room, away from the *barre*.

arabesque A beautiful balance on one leg.

assemblé A jump where the feet come together at the end.

battement dégagé A foot exercise at the *barre* to get beautiful toes.

battement tendu Another foot exercise where you stretch your foot until it points.

chassé A soft, smooth slide of the feet.

echappé This one's impossible to describe, but it's like your feet escaping from each other!

fifth position croisé When you are facing, say, the *left* corner, with your feet in fifth position, and your front foot is the *right* foot.

fouetté This step is so fast your feet are in a blur! You do it to prepare for *pirouettes*.

grand battement High kick!

jeté A spring where you land on the opposite foot. Rose loves these!

pas de bourrée Tiny little steps to the side, like a mouse.

pas de chat A cat hop from one foot to the other.

plié This is the first step we do in class. You have to bend your knees slowly and make sure your feet are turned right out, with your heels firmly planted on the floor for as long as possible.

port de bras Arm movements, which Poppy is good at.

révérence The curtsy at the end of class.

rond de jambe This is where you make a circle with your leg.

sissonne A scissor step.

sissonne en arrière A scissor step going backward. This is really hard!

sissonne en avant A scissor step going forward.

soubresaut A jump off two feet, pointing your feet hard in the air.

temps levé A step and sweep up the other leg then jump.

turnout You have to stand with your legs and feet and hips all opened out and pointing to the side, not the front. This is the most important thing in ballet that everyone learns right from the start.

Poppy's Secret Wish

Poppy loves ballet and is trying really hard
to be picked to do the exam with her best
friend, Jasmine. But when new girl Rose
crashes into class, Poppy worries that she'll
never get her secret wish.

0-7945-1294-1

Jasmine's Lucky Star

Jasmine dreams of being a famous ballerina,
but she has to hide her ambition from her
strict dad. He wants her to give up ballet
to concentrate on schoolwork, but can
Jasmine change his mind?

0-7945-1295-X

Rose's Big Decision

When Rose gets ballet lessons for her birthday,
she is surprised to find out how much fun they are.
The trouble is she loves gymnastics too, but she can't
do both. Rose has to make a big decision.
0-7945-1296-8

Dancing Princess

Visitors have come to Miss Coralie's looking
for a dancer to star in a show, so Poppy is
determined to practice as hard as she can.
But will she push herself too far?
0-7945-1297-6

Dancing with the Stars

Not only has Jasmine been invited to watch a
professional ballet class, she's also got the chance to
audition for the Royal Ballet School. But her dad
needs some convincing to let her go.
0-7945-1298-4

Dancing Forever

There's a boy in Rose's ballet class and she can't help
playing around with him and getting into trouble.
Will she blow her chances of taking her exam?
0-7945-1299-2